THE KILLING VISION

Also by
Will Overby

August

Drum

The Human Condition:
Short Fiction and Poetry

The Killing Vision

The Island

Devil's Catacombs

Moon Shadow

The Novelist

A Vision of Murder

THE KILLING VISION

WILL OVERBY

BLACK CAT BOOKS

OWENSBORO, KENTUCKY
2018

WEDNESDAY, JULY 4

9:00 PM

Although the heat had baked the ground hard and dry throughout the day, the sun had now set, leaving a layer of humidity over the town like a wet blanket. Hoards of people—some from Cedar Hill, some from other communities, a few of the students still in town at the college for summer classes—had converged on Riverside Park for the annual band concert and fireworks spectacular. Families had spread picnics over the grounds, and many were enjoying a watermelon or a cool drink in the deepening twilight, slapping away the mosquitoes that had swarmed up from the sluggish river below.

At precisely nine o'clock, the first bursts of color exploded in the velvet sky, bringing cheers from the crowd. Smaller children squealed with delight, and some of the older teenagers took advantage of the distraction to sneak off underneath the old grandstand to make out.

Missiles screamed through the sky, then erupted in showers of spinning sparks, their smoke trails extending into the darkness like the legs of giant descending spiders.   Several large explosions shook the ground; a young woman screamed with surprise, and several people with her laughed.

The booming of the fireworks echoed throughout the river valley, stirring the brackish water as well as the debris of tree limbs clawing at the shore.   With each vibrating explosion, a pile of rotting logs at the water's edge shifted a bit more until it finally broke apart and the trees drifted away, leaving a mangled, twisted bundle that floated and bobbed in the darkness.

Kelly Sutton and Mark Davis had slid down the bank away from the crowd to a small landing at the edge of the river.   Mark's plan was to get Kelly away from her parents and friends so the two of them could fool around under the fireworks.   They had been together now for a few weeks, and the time was nearing when Mark expected more than just a goodnight kiss.

Kelly repeatedly shoved Mark's groping hand away from her breasts as they kissed.   "Not here," she said.

"Why not?"

"Somebody might see."

Mark looked around.   "There's nobody else down here."   With one finger he slipped a strand of her hair out of her eyes and kissed her forehead.   "Come on."

She slid away from him slightly.   "It's too hot.   Let's wait 'til we get back to my house.   Besides, it stinks down here."

"It's just fish."

"Smells like something dead."

"Probably a 'possum or a cat or somethin'."

A large explosion over their heads made her jump, and she settled back into the crook of his arm. The boom vibrated the ground beneath them, and Kelly felt the stirring in her chest that only added to the intensity of her pounding heart. Mark kissed her lips again, and this time she kissed back. After a moment, she pulled back to catch her breath; both of their faces were slick with sweat. "Come on, let's go. It really stinks down here."

A bright flash of colors briefly illuminated something at the edge of the water. Kelly squinted at it in the sudden darkness. "What is that?"

"What?"

"There. Floating. See it?"

"Yeah." Mark grabbed a stick and scooted toward the water. He poked at the bundle, then stiffened.

"What is it?" Kelly asked. She moved up beside him.

More fireworks exploded over them, and in the flare, Kelly saw the rotted, green upturned face, its mouth yawning open in silent agony.

Kelly screamed, but her voice was lost in a barrage of erupting shells.

THURSDAY, JULY 5

6:01 AM

If he kept his eyes closed, maybe he could fool himself into thinking he was still asleep. Maybe the soft light filtering through his lids was just some sort of sleep-induced hallucination. Beside his head, the clock radio droned on in his right ear. Toby Keith.

Blindly, Joel reached out and slapped the snooze button and blessed silence filled the room. He rolled over and opened his eyes. Fuck. But today was Thursday, and that meant he only had to make it through two more days before the weekend. It had felt good having a day off yesterday, even if it had been close to a hundred degrees.

He stretched his massive frame spread-eagle across the double bed and stared at the ceiling. There were several cracks snaking across the white plaster, like tiny highways on a barren landscape. It reminded him briefly of the Martian canals. But that made him think of something else, something dark, so he pushed it from his head.

The light through the dusty curtains was subdued. It was going to rain today for sure. What was that old rhyme? *Red sky at morning, sailor take warning*, or some shit like that. Only the sky wasn't red, just gray and lifeless.

He peeked under the covers, down past his rotund belly, to his underwear. Was anything happening down there this morning? Any party in his pants today? Nope. Nothing. Limp noodle city, baby. Actually, he hadn't had an erection in so long, he could hardly remember what it felt like. Or what it looked like, for that matter. It was probably shriveled up past the point of no return. Like a fucking raisin.

He reached out and grabbed a crumpled pack of Marlboros off the bedside table, pulled one out with his gummy lips, and lit it. First one of the day. God, it felt good, sucking that sweet nicotine down inside. He placed the ashtray on his chest, the amber glass cold against his skin, and balanced the cigarette on its edge, watching the steel-blue smoke curl upward from the smoldering glow of the tip, feeling the pleasant buzz in his chest.

The radio blared on again, and the ashtray tumbled off his chest when he jumped, spilling ashes, crushed butts, and his lit cigarette across the sheets. *"Shit!"*

Gary Hamby of the WCDH morning show was just starting the news. Joel was in the midst of cleaning up the mess on the bed when he heard the report of the body they had pulled from the river last night. It was Sarah Jo McElvoy. The fourteen-year-old girl had been missing since April. Her throat had been cut.

Joel wondered briefly if he might be able to find the killer, wondered if by touching Sarah Jo's lifeless body the vision of her attacker's face would swim before him. But he knew better. The few times he had touched a dead person he had come away with nothing.

After standing in the numbing flow of the shower for ten minutes, Joel pulled on his coveralls and sat down at the kitchen table for another cigarette and a mug of black coffee.

He leaned back and stretched, feeling the soreness in his shoulders from climbing the cable tower at work the other day. He had almost asked Wade to do it; Wade was older, thirty-three, but he was in much better shape. But he knew Wade would get pissed. Wade was like that; you couldn't ask him any favors because he resented it, and he held it over your head for the rest of your life. Even if he was your older brother. Besides, climbing the tower was Joel's job.

He had been halfway up when the pain shot through his left arm, a pain so sudden and sharp he thought at first he had been stung by a hornet. But there was nothing. Sweat poured down his face, and despite his lack of fear of high places, his head spun with vertigo. His boots slipped off the tower. For a brief, horrifying moment he knew he was going to fall. He was going to plummet straight to the bottom of the ridge that held the tower. The safety equipment holding him, the same straps and buckles he barely looked at when he put them on, would fail, would break under the strain of his weight. He clinched his eyes shut and braced his body, waiting for the plunge.

But it never happened. The safety harness held, and he was able to regain his footing, resting his head against the hot metal of the tower while he tried to catch his breath.

"Hey," Wade called up to him. "Let's get on with it. It's almost time for lunch."

Joel climbed the rest of the way to the top without incident, made a great show of pretending to inspect the cables, and inched back to the bottom. He doubled over and rested his elbows on his knees as he tried to catch his breath. He fully expected Wade to lay into him for almost falling, but he didn't. Wade had apparently either not seen or didn't care.

Wade clapped him on the back. "You're gonna have to start workin' out, man," he said.

And now as he sat at the table in the dim kitchen, Joel massaged his arm and shoulder. For a while he had thought he might have suffered a light heart attack. That scared him worse than the possibility of falling to his death. But this morning he still felt sore, and he was fairly sure he had just pulled a muscle. But he was still going to find an excuse to not climb during the next tower maintenance.

* * *

When Joel pulled the cable truck into Wade's driveway, Wade was standing on the front porch, grabbing one last cigarette since they were not allowed to smoke in the company trucks. He flicked the butt out into the yard and motioned for Joel to get out.

Joel glanced at his watch as he slid out and slammed the door behind him. "We're gonna be late."

"Got something to show you," Wade said. He stepped off the porch and headed up the drive toward the old barn at the back of the house.

Joel followed hesitantly. "You didn't kill another copperhead did you?"

Wade glanced at him and grinned; he knew Joel was deathly afraid of snakes. Once when Joel was twelve and Wade was sixteen, they had found an old snakeskin out in the woods. Wade hid it in a box in the closet, and they both forgot about it. Wade found it some time later and decided to have some fun with it. Joel awoke one morning to find the skin draped over his pillow. By the time he realized it was just the old skin, he had already wet the bed in fright.

Wade pulled back the heavy weathered door and light spilled onto a shapeless mass hiding beneath a rust-stained tarp. "Got a great deal on this from a guy over in Russellville. He and his brother even drove it over here." He whipped off the tarp, and Joel sucked in his breath.

Sitting in the shadows of the barn was a red Ford Mustang convertible, its tattered top folded back. There were a couple of rust spots on the front fenders, the bumpers were tarnished, and it was missing the chrome "R" from "FORD" on the hood, but it was a Mustang just the same. Everything from the scowl of the nose to the pony emblem on the gas cap signified power. The car seemed to be in motion even though it was standing still. Joel reached out to stroke the dusty surface with his fingertips—guiltily, as if he were touching a naked woman. "What year?" he asked.

"'Sixty-five."

"How much you pay?"

"Twenty-five hundred."

Joel whistled softly, peering down the side of the car for any telltale ripples. "Needs a lotta work."

"I know." Wade was still grinning with pride. He caressed the black vinyl of the driver's seat like a lover. "You'll help me, won'tcha?"

"Sure," Joel said. He couldn't help but finger the pony emblem on the grill, tracing the galloping legs and flowing mane.

"Dad?" Wade's son was peering around the door, his dark hair sticking up in tufts.

Joel jerked his hand back reflexively, as if he had been caught doing something obscene.

Derek padded into the barn, his feet slapping against the packed bare ground. He was wearing only a pair of jeans, and his chest already had that beefy hard look that ran in the Roberts family. The kid was sixteen but big as he was he could easily pass for twenty. "When are we gonna start working on the car?"

Wade reached up to scratch underneath his cap. "Probably this weekend. Joel's gonna help."

Derek looked at Joel and smiled. "Cool."

"Derek!" came a voice from the side door of the house.

Derek blew out a breath. "Guess I'd better go."

Before he could hit the open door, Wade's wife appeared in the driveway. Marla's soft blonde hair was loose and flying about her head. Even so, Joel still thought she was beautiful. He always had. It was her eyes. They were dark and haunted, as though she had endured a great amount of tragedy. But if she had, it had not touched her loveliness. It was almost as if the more she had been tortured, the more beautiful she had become, as if God were overcompensating for her pain. Joel had never touched her, so he wasn't sure if what he believed was true, but he had never failed to be awed in her presence.

This morning, however, anger flashed in her eyes. "Derek!"

Derek slunk out of the barn toward her. "I'm coming. Jesus."

"You don't even have your shirt and shoes on. You're gonna be late for work!" Derek was working in town this summer at Dairy Queen, and Joel wondered if the boy was as lazy at work as he seemed to be at home. Marla glanced at Joel and nodded in greeting.

"Morning, Marla," he said as she slipped out of sight.

"Marla, lay off the boy for five minutes," Wade called after her. "Goddammit."

Joel looked at his watch again. "We've gotta go."

* * *

On the short drive into town, passing the plows working desperately in the fields before the rain came, Joel turned down the radio and took a quick glance at his brother. Wade sat on the passenger side, staring out at the passing land, chewing his thumbnail. "So, what did Marla say?" Joel asked.

"About what?"

"The car."

"Oh." Even though the day was dark, Wade was wearing sunglasses, which made it impossible for Joel to read his eyes when he said, "She didn't put up much of a fight."

Joel pondered this for a moment, then turned his attention back to the road. "They found that girl's body."

"Who?"

"You know. The McElvoy girl. The one that's been missing so long."

Wade nodded. "I'd forgot about her."

"They said her throat had been cut."

Beside him, Wade said, "Turn up the radio."

* * *

As they walked through the front door of the cable office, Betsy, the office manager, stood behind the counter with her arms crossed, several files in one hand. "Well," she said, "if it isn't the Roberts boys." Betsy was good at intimidating people, which was one reason she was successful in her job; in the two years since she had started, overdue accounts were down by sixty percent and employee absenteeism was almost nil. "I was wondering about you two," she said, tossing her blonde hair, which really meant, *You're late.* "Got several orders for you in the box," she said. "The other guys are already out." She headed off toward her office.

At the other end of the service counter, Rhonda Rose, the billing clerk, suppressed a snicker. All the guys in the office thought Rhonda was hot. Though only a couple of years out of high school, she possessed the confidence and aloofness of someone much older, someone who was aware of her sensuality but not driven by it. Wade talked about her sometimes, especially after he had had a few beers, going into detail about what the two of them would do in his bed if Marla wasn't around.

"You guys are in trouble," Rhonda said, stretching out the last word as if singing it.

Wade sauntered to the counter and leaned over it, propped on one elbow. "Just how much trouble are we in?" he asked, grinning.

She smiled back at him. "Plenty."

"Then you may have to punish me," he said. "Joel's on his own."

Rhonda rolled her eyes. "Whatever."

Outside, as they climbed back in the truck with their work orders, Wade whistled through his teeth. "God-damn, she's sexy. Man, wouldn't you like to have some of that?"

Joel looked away, feeling his face turn hot. "She's pretty."

Wade shook his head. "Pretty. Yeah." He slugged Joel in the arm. "You fuckin' faggot. You could probably go out with her if you wanted to."

Joel snorted. "Right. I'm every woman's dream date."

"You could clean up a little better, you know. Get a decent haircut. Shave off that fuckin' goatee." He grabbed Joel's dark whiskers and tugged. Joel shoved Wade's arm away, catching a fragment of thought from

Wade's head.

(*fat ugly*)

Joel started the truck and pulled out of the parking lot. He hated Wade when he got on these personal trainer kicks. It was bad enough knowing how unattractive you were without having your own brother reiterate it. Besides, Joel knew better than to try to get involved with anyone; he understood that when he touched someone, when he was able see them, they ceased to be appealing to him. There was something both sickening and frightening about being in another person's head. But of course, that was not anything he could tell Wade.

8:23 PM

Lieutenant Mike Halloran was standing in the city hospital morgue, watching with sickening fascination as the county medical examiner unzipped the black bag containing what remained of Sarah Jo McElvoy. Her face, the color of rotten egg yolk, was framed with matted, dirty blonde hair that brushed against the gaping, puckered tear in her throat. One eye was gone, its socket sunken and shriveled; the other gazed blankly at the ceiling, white and clouded. Her lips hung open to reveal a mouth blackened inside with river silt. But it was the stench that got him, the smell of putrefying flesh and the fishy smell of the river. The smell of death.

Halloran pulled a handkerchief out of his pocket and covered his nose and mouth. He glanced across the table at his partner, Detective John Chapman, a big strapping guy with short red hair and freckled skin. Together the two of them made up the tiny investigations unit of the Cedar Hill police department. Right now Chapman looked pale and grim as he watched the preparations for the autopsy.

The examiner, Carl Scott, whom everyone referred to as "Scotty," was a grizzled little butterball with a gray mustache, and Halloran had dealt with him often. Scotty was cutting away the remnants of Sarah Jo's t-shirt, purple with a pink cat on it, what she had been wearing when she disappeared. He pulled the cloth back to reveal the blotchy skin beneath. "She's quite bruised up," he said. He turned and scribbled some notes on a pad beside the table. "Lots of decay."

Halloran looked away. "Well, she's probably been dead three months, Scotty."

The examiner looked at him over the rims of his glasses. "Not that long."

"You sure?"

"Yep." He continued to strip away the cloth, revealing Sarah Jo's pitiful, barely developed breasts. "If she had, she'd look worse than this."

"How long, then, you think?" asked Halloran.

Scotty shrugged. "A few days. Hard to say."

Below the scraps of the t-shirt, Sarah Jo was naked. When the body had been pulled from the river, there was no sign of her jeans or underwear. Her vulva was purple and swollen, sagging open. Scotty was bent over her now, probing with his instruments and speaking into a ceiling-mounted microphone attached to a recording device. "Some bruising and tearing around the vaginal opening," he announced. "Some massive trauma to the whole area." He placed his scalpel gently on the side of the table. "She was raped," he said without emotion. "Very violently."

Halloran looked from Scotty to the body splayed out before them. He pressed the handkerchief tighter across his nose and blew out a disgusted breath. He had had all he could stand. He motioned to Chapman. "Let's get out of here," he said. "You call us if you find anything."

Scotty didn't look up. "Will do."

Outside, the evening had descended with suddenness, and the rain that had threatened all day pelted the sidewalks. Halloran and Chapman trotted to the unmarked sedan and slid inside. The air in the car was hot and thick. Halloran started the engine and put the air conditioner on full blast. They both sat there, drained, listening to the rain hammer the roof.

"I hate that," Chapman said, not looking at him. "I figured she'd been raped."

Halloran nodded. He'd expected it, too. More often than not, young teenagers who disappeared fell victim to sexual predators who regarded them as living toys to be tortured and discarded. He had hoped that Cedar Hill wasn't harboring such a beast. Even in the early stages, when it was still a missing persons case, he had told himself that that kind of thing didn't exist out here, not in such a small community.

Two days after Sarah Jo's disappearance, Halloran and Chapman were working with other law enforcement agencies (including the Lake County sheriff's department and the FBI) and volunteers, to launch a massive search operation. In addition to combing the residential and commercial districts, they had questioned a couple dozen or so kids on the Cedar Hill College campus, searched every building. It had taken weeks. Hardly any of the students at the college were commuters; most either lived in town or in the one dormitory. The college was a private school, which meant it was expensive, and most of these kids were from upscale families in this part of the state. The idea that a student (or anyone else for that matter) could have committed such an atrocious act sickened Halloran beyond words.

After a while Sarah Jo had melted into the list of missing and runaway teens, her face plastered on posters in bus stations and truck stops across the country along with countless others.

Beside him, Chapman continued to stare at the rain-washed windshield. Halloran knew Chapman had a daughter of his own, a cute little bug about two, and he wondered if he was thinking about her now, imagining her broken, lifeless body lying on a stainless steel table under the cold lights of the morgue. Halloran reached over and slapped him on the thigh. "Let's go home."

* * *

By the time Halloran reached his apartment building, the storm had intensified. Streaks of lightning illuminated the sky as the fireworks had the night before. Just inside the foyer, he wriggled out of his sopping sports jacket and grabbed his mail from the box, then trudged up the stairs toward home.

Mel was meowing on the other side of the door before the key was even in the lock. "Hey, you stupid cat," Halloran said, scooping him up. "Past dinner time, huh?" He threw his coat and the mail onto the couch and carried Mel into the kitchen, setting him on the counter. The overhead fluorescent flickered to life and Halloran pulled a can of 9 Lives from the cabinet. Mrs. Donovan, his cleaning lady, had stocked up at the grocery today, but she'd apparently forgotten to feed the cat. Mel began to purr, rubbing against Halloran's arm, then greedily dived into his dinner.

There were some Mexican leftovers in the refrigerator from Tuesday, but he didn't think he could stomach that tonight. Nothing really sounded appealing. He opened a beer and swallowed a third of it in one drink, then pulled a cigarette from the pack in his shirt pocket.

He loosened his tie as he shuffled down the hall, the unlit cigarette dangling from his lips. In the dark bedroom, he stepped out of his shoes and stretched out on the bed, wriggling his toes. He reached for his lighter and lit his cigarette. What a terrible twenty-four hours this had been.

He tried to imagine Chapman at home with his wife and kid across town. There he was at thirty with everything Halloran still wanted at forty. A family. A house. Someone to come home to. Chapman had joined the department right after high school. His father had been a cop in a neighboring county, so Chapman had practically grown up in the force. It had seemed to be his destiny.

Halloran on the other hand had knocked about for a couple of years after graduating from college, first working as a manager for a firm that owned several convenience stores before joining the police department in Cedar Hill. He'd truly enjoyed most of the work he did as a cop, though he had to admit there were some rough moments. He had been shot at, spat on, kicked, slapped, punched, and called everything imaginable. After a couple of years he had been promoted to detective. His first partner was a mean son-of-a-bitch named Logan who retired a year later and was replaced with Mark Miller. Miller was a guy just a couple of years older than Halloran, and the two of them had formed an instant bond; in fact, they often hung out together outside work, even taking a couple of weekend fishing trips over at the lakes. But last year Miller had decided to move out west—big-sky country. Halloran, now a lieutenant, was placed in charge of investigations and Chapman had been brought up from the ranks to fill his old slot. Although they got along well, Chapman wasn't the kind of guy to hang around after quitting time. Chapman had his little family to go home to, and he wasn't interested in kicking back for an after-work beer or taking off for a long weekend. Marriage certainly changed things, and in spite of his loneliness sometimes, Halloran was grateful to not have that baggage on him.

Not that he hadn't had chances. There had been several women in and out of his life over the years, and one or two that he had briefly considered marrying. But the nature of his work kept him from getting in too deep with anyone. After observing day in and day out what people did to each other, you got a kind of apathy toward life. You learned to turn off that part of yourself that needed an emotional attachment. You became an animal of sorts—eating, sleeping, working. And once a woman realized that about you, she gave up and moved on to something else. Besides, the crazy hours he worked didn't leave him much time for a social life.

He took a swig of his beer and felt the coldness spread through his belly. Christ, when was the last time he'd been with a woman? Eight months? A year? He couldn't remember. Occasionally he found himself sniffing around after Camron, the dispatcher at the station; she was Hispanic—dark-skinned and green-eyed with legs that looked as though they might squeeze the breath out of you if they were wrapped around your waist. He smiled at that; when he fantasized, he usually thought of Camron. Lonely as he sometimes was though, women just complicated things. Period. As jealous as he might be of John Chapman, he knew he was happier the way he was.

No commitments. That was the way to go. He drank to it.

The cell phone rang next to his bed, and he picked it up after the first ring.

"Mike? It's Scotty."

Halloran took a drag off his cigarette. "What'cha got?"

"Well, she was strangled before her throat was cut."

Halloran blew out a stream of smoke. "Christ."

"And there's something else. I've been looking at

some tissue samples..."

"Yeah?"

"I've never seen anything like it. I'm gonna call in my friend from the state, have him come take a look just to be sure."

Damn, Scotty could be vague sometimes. "For God's sake, Scotty, what're you talking about?"

Scotty's voice was hard. "I was wrong about the time of death. She's probably been dead for quite a while—maybe since she disappeared. But she's only been exposed for about four days. That's based on insect larva found in her mouth and other orifices."

Halloran clinched his teeth on the butt of the cigarette. "What are you saying, Scotty?"

"Her body's been kept refrigerated. Probably frozen."

FRIDAY, JULY 6

3:23 AM

Joel sat in the dilapidated recliner in the living room, watching the lightning flash outside. An hour ago, the power had gone out, leaving the house in utter darkness. He had awoke in the sudden blackness and fumbled for the battery-powered weather radio in the bedside drawer, and when he was sure there were no tornadoes heading his way, he tried to go back to sleep. But the crashing thunder kept rousing him, and he finally got out of bed and shuffled to the living room to wait out the storm.

Sometimes he wished during one of these big storms that the wind would just suck up this house where he had grown up and everything in it—the furniture, the knick-knacks, the memories. He hated the place. He hated the old life it represented, the way things were before his mother and stepfather got killed. It was as if the house had held on to all the hate and oppression and now leached it back out like some deadly radiation, a force that had weakened him so that he could never get away from it.

Mama and his stepfather Clifton had been dead for five years now. They had been killed when Clifton had pulled in front a train at a crossing in town. The stupid bastard. He had been trying to outrun it, to save a couple of minutes, but he had misjudged the distance. The freight train, hauling seventy-three loaded coal cars, had slammed into the pickup truck and dragged it a mile before it could stop. Mama and Clifton were both dead at the scene.

In a way, it was a relief. The fucker was dead. He could never hurt anyone anymore.

Clifton Roberts had come into their lives when Joel was three and Wade was seven. Their real father, Paul Coffman, had died a year earlier in a mining accident. Mama seemed to waste no time in finding another man; hell, she knew she *needed* a man if she and the boys were to survive. She and Clifton dated a few weeks and were married one day on Clifton's lunch hour. By the time she discovered the monster he really was, he had already adopted the boys and taken control of all their lives. It was too late.

When Joel was ten, Clifton lost his job at the quarry. As time passed with no other job prospects in sight and money becoming tighter, Clifton grew increasingly irritable, increasingly violent. Any cross word or transgression by the boys, no matter how unintentional, resulted in immediate and merciless punishment.

Clifton's favorite method was surprise. He would

come at you without warning, without any indication that you were a target. The first time Joel could remember was when he had spilled his milk at the dinner table. Clifton stood up and slapped Joel so hard that he fell out of his chair.

"Clean that mess up," Clifton spat. "You know how expensive milk is. We're barely makin' it, and you go spill all that."

With the side of his head stinging in pain, Joel got to his feet and grabbed a dishcloth from the kitchen counter. He sopped at the milk, tears streaming down his cheeks.

"Stop that goddamn blubberin'."

Carefully, Joel wiped up the rest of the milk.

"Now sit down and eat."

Joel looked at his empty glass. "Can I get some more milk?"

Rage flared in Clifton's eyes. "Hell, no. You're gonna have to do without."

The hatred, the anger in that voice pierced Joel to his very core, and the tears started up again.

Suddenly, Clifton was on his feet, pulling his belt from around his waist. "I said *stop that!*" The belt came cutting through the air with a whistle, striking the side of Joel's head. He screamed and fell to the floor. He lay on the hard floor like a slug, his mind spinning toward a circle of black. Mama had not moved an inch, had not uttered a word of protest.

When Clifton found work, the tension over money subsided, but Clifton's violence remained. Wade and Joel were often whipped with the belt, sometimes so hard that whelps were left on their skin for days.

Joel began to put on weight in his teens; he'd never understood why, since he was active and healthy. In any event, Clifton's random punishments grew more frequent, more violent. Clifton seemed to hate the sight of him.

Not long after his sixteenth birthday, Joel was heading through the house toward his room when Clifton grabbed his arm. It had been almost a year since he'd discovered his strange ability, and Joel had learned to steel himself against the torrent of sensation, both physical and mental. Most of his encounters were the result of accidentally brushing into someone, catching a fleeting thought like a short blast from a passing radio. This was different.

The sensations rushing through him from Clifton were black and brutal, a wave of hatred so strong it nearly knocked Joel to the floor. A roar flooded his head, a mixture of screams both male and female that morphed into one agonizing wail that was asexual and almost harmonic, terrifying yet strangely beautiful. Images streaked past his vision—blood and naked limbs, Mama's face twisted in agony. Then, somewhere in the midst of the seizure, a tiny spark of pain ignited and began to grow. It loomed before him, drowning out all his other senses, a pain so intense, so sickening that it penetrated every fiber of his being. And then the words exploded into his head, Clifton's voice yet not Clifton's voice but the voice of the devil (*YOU FILTHY STINKIN' PIG FUCKIN' QUEER BASTARD SHOW YOU HOW FAT QUEERS LIKE IT*) and the pain! The pain was excruciating. And then he realized that Clifton was gripping his testicles, crushing his balls in his filthy, nicotine-stained fingers and Joel was screaming and crying but there was no one there. Mama was gone. Wade was gone. They were alone in the house.

And then, miraculously, Clifton let go, leaving Joel to writhe on the floor in pain, clutching his bruised testicles as wave after wave of nausea washed over him. He fought against the urge to vomit. Clifton was looming over him, his voice drawn out and slow as he said, "The next time you play with yourself, I'll cut the goddamn thing off." He stomped out of the room, his worn leather workboots scuffing the wood floor.

Joel did not know what to think. It was the one incident he had never spoken to anyone about.

Throughout all of this time, through all of Clifton's violent and unexpected outbursts, Mama seemed to ignore everything. Joel had hugged her once after he attained his ability and saw that she was deathly afraid of Clifton. She was terrified of what he might do to the boys, but she was more fearful of what he would do to *her*. He had seen everything—unspeakable acts of perversion in the solace of their bedroom, sudden eruptions of anger and humiliation—all directed at her. He had been simultaneously outraged and sickened. Though at first he couldn't understand why their mother refused to take up for them, he finally understood. It was all there in her head. She was afraid he would kill her, *knew* he would kill her if she dared take a stand against him.

He had wondered countless times how different things would have been had their real father not died, if

Clifton had never shown up to tear their lives to shreds. But it was pointless to think about that. The past was the past, and there was nothing about it that could be changed.

Now, as the lightning flashed and the thunder grew distant, Joel lit a cigarette and let it smolder in the blackness, dangling from his fingers, his feet drawn up in the chair. He was not surprised that his cheeks were wet with tears. He rarely thought of Clifton without crying.

He sucked on the cigarette and stared at the blackness outside the windows. The rain had stopped, but the lightning continued to flash, brilliant bursts of light that showed the sky to be a whirling, boiling gray mass.

10:45 AM

"All right, so explain this to me again."

Scotty swiped a sweaty fan of gray hair off his forehead and laid a computer-printed photograph on top of the clutter on his desk. "This is a microscopic picture of the McElvoy girl's skin cells. The tissue is damaged. Not in a normal way. This is how cells look after a body has been subjected to extremely cold temperatures. The kind of cells we find when somebody's frozen to death, after the cells have died and then thawed."

Halloran shot a glance at Chapman, then looked back at Scotty. "But the temperature hasn't been below sixty probably since she disappeared."

"I know."

Chapman took the picture of the cells from Halloran and studied it. The reddish-pink ovals were ringed with rough brown outlines. "So are you saying that somebody killed this girl, kept her body frozen, and then just dumped her in the river a couple of days ago?"

"So it would seem."

"For what purpose?"

Scott shrugged. "Who knows?"

Halloran blew out a breath and reached for his cigarettes.

"You know you can't smoke in here, Mike," said Scotty.

"Come on," Halloran said, cramming the pack back into his shirt pocket, "you're stressing me out here. Don't you have anything else that might help us?"

Scotty shook his head. "I wish I had more. There's not even anything under her fingernails. They've been scraped. Probably by whoever killed her."

Chapman leaned forward. "Any prints from where she was strangled?"

"No. Perp wore gloves, apparently. I tried to determine the size of his hands from the bruises, but that was inconclusive."

"What about DNA?" asked Halloran. "Any saliva? Surely there's blood or semen."

"Nothing." He stopped.

"What?"

Scotty cleared his throat. "She was violated with some object. Something blunt and wooden. There were splinters in the vaginal walls. It was done after she was dead."

Chapman blew out a sigh. Halloran glanced at him, then stared above Scotty's head at the anatomical charts on the wall. "Do you think that this guy kept her for a while so he could..." He couldn't bring himself to say what he was imagining.

"Yes," Scotty said without hesitation. "That's exactly what I think."

Halloran rubbed his dry lips, wanting—*needing*—a smoke. "Holy Christ."

11:35 AM

Marla sat at the kitchen table, staring out the screen door to the back yard, across the overgrown field, to the woods beyond. Before her sat a full, untouched cup of lukewarm coffee. Beside it a small piece of notepaper lay unfolded displaying a penciled phone number. On top of the paper, holding it flat, was Wade's Smith & Wesson thirty-eight revolver, fully loaded.

She had found the paper accidentally this morning while doing the laundry, routinely checking pockets as she always did. She had pulled out the note and laid it in the stack with the coins and other objects she had found in Wade's and Derek's clothes, not really paying attention to it until after she had started the washer and began sorting through the discarded items. There was almost a dollar in change, some wadded gum wrappers, a crumpled pack of cigarettes, Wade's container of Skoal he was always misplacing, and the note.

She unfolded the note and stared at it for a second. *555-8344 Missy.* A girl's writing. At first, she thought she must be confused, that the note had come from one of Derek's pockets. But she remembered pulling it from Wade's work pants. She smoothed it out on top of the dryer. *Missy.*

At first she was numb, trying to decipher it like it was some secret code. And when she realized it was a phone number, she felt the first sparks of hurt and anger. But not surprise.

She carried the note up to the kitchen and dialed the number, and when a groggy, young female voice answered, Marla said, "Is this Missy?"

"Yeah."

"Hi, Missy. This is Wade Roberts's wife."

The line went dead.

It wasn't as if this had been the first time. Wade had been cheating on her for years, practically since they had been married. The few times she had confronted him, he had at first denied it, then admitted it. Then flaunted it. Then punished her for it.

At first she thought maybe she *was* to blame, that if only she were a little more inventive, a little less prudish, a little more willing to give him the things he wanted... And gradually she began to understand that it didn't matter. No matter how much she did for him, he would want something different, more and more extreme. He would want to push the envelope. That was one of his favorite expressions. "That Dale Earnhardt— he knew how to *push the envelope*." Or, "Come on, baby, let's *push the envelope* tonight." Once, when they had been married just a few months, he had pushed the envelope too far, and she had bled

for two days. After that, she started to become unavail-
able. Always sleepy. Or sick to her stomach. Not that
she had to pretend to be reviled by him; the thought of
his touch was enough to revolt her, to disgust her. Little by little, he asked her for it less often, and by the
time she realized what was happening, it was too late.
She had pushed him away. Driven him to the sluts and
whores he now used to satisfy himself.

They had been married two years when she found
the first evidence. She had gone out to the old Buick
for the checkbook (she was always leaving it in the
glove box), and when she opened the driver door,
something peeking from beneath the back seat caught
her eye. She pulled it out and stared at it. It was a pair
of pink panties with a lacey waistband. A size smaller
than her own.

That night, when Wade returned home from work
and two-year-old Derek was safely in front of the TV in
the other room, she flung the panties onto the dining
room table. Wade was nursing his second beer of the
evening, and it took him a moment to register what he
was seeing in front of him. He stared at them. Took
another sip of beer.

"Whose are those?" Marla said, her voice quivering
with anger.

He looked at her, his gaze steady. "None of your
goddamn business."

Her breath left her, and she stared at him. "It *is* my
goddamned business. If somebody else is fucking my
husband, I want to know who it is."

She never saw the fist coming until it connected with

her jaw. She was suddenly sitting in the floor, dazed, the room spinning away, blood dripping from her mouth. She held out both hands to steady herself, not believing he had actually punched her. She moved her tongue, not surprised to discover that a couple of her teeth were loose.

He towered above her, his chest heaving. "I said it's none of your goddamned business."

Later, when he rolled into bed beside her, he said softly, "I'm sorry. But you hardly ever let me touch you anymore." She lay there with her back to him, silent. In a few minutes, he was snoring, and she realized she had been holding her body rigid since he had come into the room.

It was not the last time he exploded. Over the years she had learned to stay out of his way, to not provoke him. She had learned how to hide bruises and cuts, how to lie about how clumsy she was and how she kept bumping into things. She had learned how to pretend everything was *fine*. People were always asking how she was—at church, at the supermarket; she learned how to say, "*Fine*." She could even smile when she said it.

There had been a few times when she thought of leaving, when she thought of driving away some day while he was at work, but she knew she could never do that. She couldn't do that to Derek. As much as she feared Wade, she knew she was the only buffer between his temper and their son, and if she weren't there to take the blows, Derek would be the only other target. And even though he was a big kid, more than capable of defending himself, she did not want to put him in that position.

And what kind of life could she make on her own? She was a high-school dropout with no marketable skills and no money of her own. What little she had managed to save (socked away for Derek's college education), the asshole had blown on that damned Mustang.

She knew she certainly couldn't go back to her parents; they had made that perfectly clear when she became pregnant. "If you're gonna lay with a dog, you gotta live with his fleas," her father had told her.

But she *did* have a choice. She looked at the gun and took a sip of coffee, not tasting it. She could be ready when he came home. She could be sitting right here at the table, pointing it at him when he came through the back door. She could shoot him right between the eyes and he would never know what had hit him. She could already see the blood and brains sprayed all over the walls and the window. It would be one mess she wouldn't mind cleaning up.

But she might miss. And if she did... If she missed, God help her. He would kill her. She had no doubt about that. There would be no hope for either her or Derek then.

She rested her head on her hands and wept.

3:35 PM

Sarah Jo McElvoy's mother was not doing well today. Not well at all.

She met Halloran and Chapman at the door with red eyes and tousled hair, looking like she hadn't slept in days and smelling faintly of whiskey. She made no move to let them in, said nothing to them as she looked at them blankly. She had been forty when Sarah Jo had been born, Halloran remembered her telling them, which would make her fifty-four now, but she looked at least seventy this afternoon.

Halloran licked his dry lips. "Mrs. McElvoy?"

"What do you want?"

"I'm Detective Mike Halloran," he said, holding up his badge. "This is my partner, John Chapman. Remember us?"

She continued to stare at them.

"May we come in and talk with you for a minute?"

She moved aside and they stepped into the dark house.

The living room was dusty and cluttered and smelled of stale cigarette smoke and cat urine. Halloran took a seat on a ragged sofa, and Chapman sat tentatively beside him. Mrs. McElvoy slumped into a grimy vinyl recliner opposite them and continued to stare.

Halloran swallowed and took a memo pad from his shirt pocket. She was beginning to unnerve him with her glazed expression. "First of all," he said, "I just want to let you know how sorry we are for—"

"You caught him yet?"

Halloran looked up at her. "Excuse me?"

"The bastard that killed my little girl. Have you caught him yet?"

Halloran managed a grim sympathetic smile. "Not

yet."

Mrs. McElvoy was shaking her head. "Sumbitch is gonna pay. He's gonna pay for what he did to Sarah Jo."

Halloran glanced at Chapman, then leafed through his notepad. "Mrs. McElvoy, when Sarah Jo first disappeared, you told us that you didn't know anyone who might have taken her. Is that still the case?"

She looked at him squarely. "I don't know anybody that would have wanted to hurt Sarah Jo." One tear, fat and round, squeezed from her eye and slid silently down her lined cheek. "She was sweet. Such a sweet girl."

"What about Sarah Jo's father? Have you heard anything from him? The last time we talked to you, you said you hadn't spoken to him. Has any of that changed since..." He started to say "since the body was found," but decided that was a bit cold; the poor woman was just now coming to grips with the fact that her daughter was officially dead, not just missing. He cleared his throat. "Has he contacted you since Sarah Jo was found?"

She shook her head. "Haven't heard from the sumbitch in seven years. Don't expect to now."

Halloran glanced around the cluttered room. Pictures of Sarah Jo lined a shelf along one wall. One of them—the same photograph that had been repeatedly plastered in shop windows and left to fade on telephone poles the last three months—showed a smiling, fresh-faced girl on the verge of womanhood, her large blue eyes staring into the camera lens into infinity, into the unlucky and damnable fate that awaited her. Chapman was staring at it, too, and Halloran quickly looked back at his notepad.

"Mrs. McElvoy," said Chapman, "just now you said 'that bastard.' Do you think it's a man?"

She snorted, a wretched, ugly sound. "It's always a man, ain't it? Ain't no woman that would kill a little girl and leave her floatin' in the river. Ain't no woman alive would do that."

Halloran folded up his memo pad and stuffed it back into his pocket, glancing about the house. "Mrs. McElvoy, do you have anyone staying with you? Any family?"

"Nope."

"Friends?"

"Nope. They've come by and stayed for a bit, but I sent them on home. Ain't nothin' they can do."

"Do you want us to send someone over for you? A counselor or anyone?"

She shook her head. "I'll tell you what I told everybody else. I just want to be left alone now. I want to be by myself. Just let me grieve in private."

He nodded, then rose from the sofa. Chapman, taking the cue, practically leaped to his feet. "We'll be in touch," Halloran told her. "Call us if anything changes."

He made to give her a reassuring touch on the shoulder as he passed, and she grabbed his arm. She looked up at him with pleading, dazed eyes. "Tell me one thing before you go. Tell me the truth. I want to know. I *need* to know."

"Yes, ma'am?"

She swallowed and looked away. "Was...was she raped?"

He saw no reason to keep it from her. "Yes, ma'am, she was. In a manner of speaking. She was violated with an object."

Mrs. McElvoy, nodded, tears flowing freely down her cheeks now, her face contorted with agony. He patted her shoulder, and Chapman followed him out the door.

Outside, last night's rain had made the heat more intense, the air heavy. Halloran's forehead broke into an instant sweat. They reached the sedan, and he was just opening his door when Mrs. McElvoy's voice surprised him. "She was comin' home from band practice, you know."

"Excuse me?"

She stood on the front porch, leaning against one of the peeling posts, her arms crossed over her chest. "The day she disappeared. She had band practice after school. She left the schoolhouse walking. Like she always did."

Halloran nodded. He remembered writing that in the report himself. "She always walked past the water treatment plant and up by the cemetery, didn't she?"

Mrs. McElvoy wasn't listening to him. She was gazing at the sky. "She played clarinet." She looked at him abruptly. "Did you ever find her clarinet?"

Halloran shook his head. "No, ma'am."

Without another word, Mrs. McElvoy turned and disappeared into the house.

Halloran blew out a breath. It would be a two-beer night.

5:22 PM

When Joel dropped him off at home, Wade pulled the pack of Winstons from his shirt pocket, stuck one between his lips, and lit it. It was the first thing he did every afternoon when he got out of the truck, since the company wouldn't let them smoke in the goddamn thing. Like it was made of gold or something.

He stood for a moment in the front yard, savoring the taste of the nicotine and the humid weight of the afternoon air. Part of him didn't want to go inside, even though his stomach was growling for dinner. He just didn't want to look at Marla today, listen to her bitch and complain, see whatever stupid thing she'd done today. He really just did not want to deal with it.

He walked past the house and down to the barn. Inside, he stripped the cover off the Mustang and looked at it. Ran his hands over the hood. He'd wanted one of these for so long, he could hardly believe he now owned one. A muscle car—that's what it was, plain and simple. Like a body builder without one ounce of fat on him. Pure power.

Marla had sure bitched when he bought the thing. God, how she had bitched. But one pop to the mouth had shut her up.

His plan was to get the Mustang restored in time for Derek's high school graduation. It sure would be a hell of a present. He could picture it parked out behind the house, all freshly-waxed and shimmering, with a big bow tied around it, and the look in Derek's eyes when Wade dropped the keys in his hand, knowing how hard they had all worked on it together.

Maybe it would help the kid grow up, help him become more of a man. He sure as shit hoped so. His greatest fear was that Derek would grow up to be a faggot. That was just something he would not be able to live with. Hell, the kid was sixteen and still hadn't ever had a girlfriend. Derek was a big kid. And good looking, too. He should have been surrounded by girls.

Wade sure as hell didn't want Derek to turn out like Joel. Now there was a pathetic bastard. Twenty-nine years old, still living by himself, mooning over girls he couldn't have, eating himself into an early grave. A freewheeling bachelor, able to play the field with as many women as he wanted, yet living alone without even a fucking dog to keep him company. The poor ugly son-of-a-bitch had never had much luck with women, though, even in high school when he played football. But now that he was older and fatter and losing his hair, well… Wade knew he probably couldn't get laid unless he paid for it.

Wade had never had a problem getting women, even as a zit-faced teenager. They just seemed to naturally flock to him. He knew he had the charm to make them feel special, to make them feel *wanted*. Hell, all he had to do was start talking to a woman and she practically melted all over the floor. Just a rare talent, he had decided.

Derek had been born when Wade was seventeen and

Marla was sixteen. They were hurriedly married at Shy Flat Church, and then they moved into a mouse-infested trailer in the back yard of Marla's parents' house. Derek was born six months later. Wade had settled down for a little while and tried to be content with just one woman. That didn't last long. Before their first anniversary he was already restless and bored, and before their second he had already slept with three other women. It wasn't that he didn't love Marla. He truly did back then. But there were times when what she could give him just wasn't enough, or didn't excite him, or couldn't satisfy him. He needed variety, and Marla just wasn't capable of providing it. And over the past few years Marla didn't seem capable of providing *anything*. They never kissed, barely touched. Sex seemed to disgust her, and now he found fulfillment exclusively outside.

This job with the cable company provided him with ample opportunities to meet women, like some of those college babes lounging around fingering each other in the dorm or bored housewives whose husbands were at work and they were home alone just waiting for the cable guy to come install HBO. Joel was usually with him on installs, but occasionally he had the good fortune to be alone, and more than once he had been shown the kind of gratitude customers didn't normally give their cable-TV installers. Most times he simply flirted, got a girl's phone number, promised to call her, that kind of thing.

Like yesterday. Joel was doing some maintenance at the office and Wade was doing an upgrade by himself at one of the apartment houses in town. He had gone around in back of the building to check the service entrance, back beside the pool. There was a girl stretched out on one of the metal chaise lounges beside the blue water, spread out during one of the few intense breaks in the threatening clouds. He had immediately begun to sweat. The fluorescent orange of her bikini was a sharp contrast to her sun-bronzed skin and long dark hair, and the mounds of her breasts splayed out from beneath the edges of her top, her nipples pressing against the material like pointing fingers. She was wearing sunglasses, so it was impossible to see her eyes, but he smiled at her anyway, and when she smiled back, he knew she was watching him as closely as he was watching her.

When he had finished his work, he made his way over to her, leaning against the wrought-iron fence that surrounded the pool area. "Hot day," he said. "Gonna storm later."

She rolled over and smiled at him. "I love the heat," she said.

Wade was looking at her breasts, at the minute droplets of perspiration that trickled between them. He licked his lips. "Guess it's not so bad if you got a pool," he said. He placed his hands on the top of the railing, knowing she would look at his left one, looking for a wedding band that wouldn't be there because he never wore one.

"I'm Missy," she said.

"Wade Roberts."

"Maybe you could come over and swim sometime. It's okay if you're a guest of a tenant."

He nodded, feeling the bulge of his erection press against the hot metal. "I'd like that." He looked around, hoping no one could see him practically humping the fence. "This what you do all day? Hang out by the pool?"

She laughed. "Not every day. I'm on vacation this week."

"Oh." He was making small talk, using any excuse he could to stand there looking at her glistening skin and the nipples poking against her bikini top. "I had you pegged for a student. Where you work?"

"I work for Dr. Seaver, the pediatrician. You know him?"

"'Fraid not."

"Don't have to ask what you do."

He grinned at her, using that full-toothed smile that always got a woman's juices flowing. "Hey, can I get your phone number?" He pulled a memo pad and a pencil from his shirt pocket and held them out to her. She took them and scribbled on the paper. *555-8344 Missy.* "Great," he said, tearing off the sheet and folding it into the pocket of his pants. "I'll give you a call. Take you up on that pool offer."

"Sounds good," she said.

By the time he returned to the truck, his zipper was just about bursting open. He drove to a secluded spot in town and took care of himself. It was quick. There might be a no-smoking rule for the company truck, but nothing said he couldn't jack off in it.

And as he thought about it now, about the orange swimsuit that barely concealed Missy's golden curves, he felt himself grow stiff again. Ignoring it, he pulled the tarp back over the Mustang and closed up the barn.

He was just crossing the yard toward the house when Derek came flying up the driveway and roared to a halt on his four-wheeler. "You better slow down," Wade told him. "You'll end up in orbit."

Derek grinned at him and hopped off the Yamaha, running a shirtsleeve across his sweaty forehead. "Ready for dinner," he said.

"Where you been?"

Derek shrugged. "Just toolin' around. Went through the woods into town, went by Chad's house to see if he was home."

"Was he?" Chad was Derek's best friend—just about his *only* friend, so far as Wade knew. They hung out together sometimes, went camping out in the woods behind the barn, fishing down at the creek—all the shit boys usually do.

"Nope. His mom said he'd gone off with his dad somewhere."

Wade grunted as they stepped up on the porch and he opened the back door. "You be careful riding that thing in town. It's illegal, you know."

"I didn't get on the streets," Derek said. "I went the back way, up through the woods, then through the park right up to his back door."

"Still," said Wade, "I don't want to have to come bail you out of jail."

"You think Chad could help us with the Mustang?" Derek asked.

"I don't know," Wade told him. "I was hopin' just

you and me would work on it. Maybe Joel."

Derek nodded and slipped into the kitchen. "That's cool."

Inside, Marla stood at the stove, frying hamburger patties in an iron skillet. Derek peeked at them, then bounded off toward the living room.

Wade looked at her. "Hey," he said.

She turned toward him and gave him an empty gaze, then turned back to the skillet. "Hey."

SATURDAY, JULY 7

5:24 AM

Halloran came slowly awake in the early gray light, coming out of a dream in which Sarah Jo McElvoy's mother was chasing him through the darkness of an inner-city alley. She was screaming at him. *"You bastard! Look what you did to my daughter! My beautiful daughter!"* He turned and saw that she was wielding an ax, and he knew she intended to kill him with it. He had just reached the dead end of the alley and had turned to brace himself for the blow when he discovered that Mrs. McElvoy had turned into Sarah Jo. Not the smiling, fresh-faced Sarah Jo from the photographs, but the rotted, blackened corpse from the morgue. She shuffled toward him, like something from a bad horror movie, her hair slimy and dripping, her eyes white and glazed, her skin a yellowish green. She was wearing the purple shirt with the cat on it, and the rest of her body was bare. "See me?" she said in a voice that sounded like dry leaves crunching together. "See me?"

At that point he became aware of the weight of the covers on his chest, and the purring cat by his face. He opened his eyes toward the blank ceiling. Mel meowed softly, then stretched. Halloran glanced over at him. "Hello, you stupid cat."

He yawned and lay there silently, remembering the dream, listening to the voice still echoing through his head. *See me?* He shivered, pulling the sheet up to his neck. Where the hell had *that* come from? He closed his eyes trying to summon back his sleep, but beside him, Mel had decided it was bath time and was noisily licking and purring.

Halloran pulled himself out of bed, pulled a pair of boxers out of the bureau drawer and padded nude across the hall to the bathroom. He took a long, loud piss, watching himself in the mirror as he did so, noticing how his stomach, once lean and flat, had begun to pooch over the last couple of years. It was what his late dad had referred to as "Dicky-do Disease," because, he said, "My belly hangs out farther than my dicky do."

He pulled on his boxers and headed toward the front door. He slid the chain from the slot and reached out into the hallway for his morning paper, then made his way through the dark living room toward the kitchen. While his coffee brewed, he unfolded the paper on the table, blew out a breath and stared down at the top story:

STILL NO SUSPECTS IN GIRL'S MURDER

Officials said Friday there are still no leads in the murder of 14-year-old Sarah Jo McElvoy of Cedar Hill.

Police Chief Norman Pettus said the investigation is proceeding "as well as can be expected," although there are currently no suspects and no apparent motive. The young girl's body was pulled from Cedar Hill's Riverside Landing on Red River July 4.

Pettus declined to comment on whether McElvoy had been sexually assaulted, but sources close to the Cedar Hill police department said the girl had been violated by a blunt wooden object.

Halloran pounded his fist on the table. "Shit." He had tried hard to keep that fact out of the paper, but someone in the police department was always willing to talk, especially when gory details were involved. At least there was no mention of the body being frozen. He could only imagine what kind of alarm that would set off in the community.

He folded up the paper and tossed it aside, then poured himself a cup of coffee. He stood at the counter, sipping it, then set his cup down. His briefcase was in the corner by the refrigerator. He reached for it, then plopped it down on the table and pulled out the file on Sarah Jo McElvoy.

In the back of the folder, tucked inside a large manila envelope, were the crime-scene photos from

Wednesday night. He pulled them out and spread them over the table.

There really wasn't much to see. The girl's body was half on the dirt shore, half in the river, surrounded by piles of rotting tree limbs that had apparently been used to hide her. Close-ups of the body revealed the putrefying skin bloated over the bones, hellish and gruesome. The dirt of the riverbank was covered in shoe prints; probably dozens of people had been along the landing that day, and who knew how many since the body had been placed there, and the freshest prints were those of the Davis boy and his girlfriend. How many times had that very place been searched since April? At least three times that he knew of. When had someone taken the body down there and concealed it under a pile of rotting limbs? And why? And who?

Another envelope in the file contained the photos from the autopsy, which he had just received yesterday from Scotty. Several of the pictures showed close-ups of the throat wound from different angles, but again there was not much to look at. In one photo, a measuring tape showed the slit to be a little over six inches long.

See me?

A sudden chill rattled him. He shoved the pictures back into the envelopes, then locked the file back in his briefcase. It was too early in the morning for this shit. Way too early. He rubbed his blurry eyes.

He couldn't shake the feeling that he was missing something. Something important. And he didn't believe he would find it in the file.

11:43 AM

Joel pulled his Explorer onto the highway and headed in toward town. There were several things he needed at Walmart, chief among them coffee and cigarettes. It was kind of sad when your very existence revolved around such things. He sucked on the Marlboro between his lips, savoring the flavor of the smoke as it rolled over his tongue and down his throat. Oh, well. Things could always be worse. At least it was a bright sunny day, Luke Bryan was on the radio, and his pack of smokes was still half full. Yeah, things could always be a lot worse.

Almost as an afterthought, he decided he would stop by Wade's before he made it all the way into Cedar Hill. Perhaps they might work on the Mustang this afternoon, and Joel could always pick up something while he was in town.

He pulled into the driveway, his wheels crunching on the dry gravel. Wade sat on the edge of the front porch, wearing only a pair of cutoff denim shorts. Beside him was an opened can of Budweiser. Shit. He knew what an asshole Wade could be when he was drinking, and he wondered if stopping was such a good idea.

Joel stepped out of the truck and flicked away the butt of his cigarette. "'Morning."

Wade looked up at him with red eyes. He was unshaven and his curly hair was matted against his head. "Hey."

Joel walked over and slumped down beside him. "Looks like you had a rough night." He barely got the words out before the smell hit him—a mixture of stale beer and sweat. And something else.

Wade gave him a crooked smile. "Up late last night." He glanced at Joel's shirt pocket. "Can I bum a smoke?"

Joel handed him the pack with the lighter stuffed inside the cellophane wrapper. "You okay?"

Wade nodded, lighting up and blowing out a plume of smoke. "I'm all right."

"Where is everybody?"

Wade motioned toward the house. "Marla's in there. Derek's at work."

Joel looked away, toward the highway. An old rusted pickup was passing by; the driver—someone he didn't recognize—waved, and Joel threw up his hand. "I'm on my way into town. Thought if you needed anything I'd pick it up for you."

"Nah."

"Thought you might need something for the Mustang. Did you want to work on it today?"

Wade took a sip of his beer, staring at the ground between his feet. He blinked, then looked at Joel. "What?"

Joel studied him. Something wasn't quite right. He thought briefly of touching him, just putting a hand on his shoulder in a gesture of brotherly concern. He would be able to tell almost instantly. But he didn't. He couldn't. The thought of seeing and how much it would drain him was too overwhelming. "I said, do you want to work on the Mustang today? I can pick up something for it while I'm in town if you need me to."

Wade shook his head. "Nah. Not today." He took another drag off the Marlboro.

"You sure you're all right?" Joel said.

Wade looked away, toward the fields across the road. "Yeah, I'm sure."

Joel stood up and pretended to yawn and stretch, feigning indifference. He didn't want to appear worried; that tended to piss Wade off, especially when he was half-lit. "Well," he said, "I'm going on. Call me later if you change your mind."

Wade nodded. "See ya."

Joel was at the first stoplight in town when it finally hit him that the underlying smell he had noticed was pot. The son-of-a-bitch had been high.

It certainly wasn't the first time he'd seen Wade stoned. Hell, in younger years the two of them had occasionally smoked some weed together. But Wade hadn't just been stoned today, he'd been fucking loopy. Half out of his head. Joel wondered what else Wade had been on. He almost wished now he had touched him, just to know. He supposed it was possible Wade was into something else, something harder, and it gave him a spark of anger and concern. He'd never known Wade to do anything but an occasional joint, but that didn't mean jack shit. People did all kinds of crazy things to fuck themselves up, and Wade was no exception.

Behind him, a horn bleeped impatiently, and Joel looked up to see the light had changed to green. He gave an apologetic wave to his rearview mirror and sped on through the intersection.

12:05 PM

Wade watched Joel roll out of the driveway. His vision swam; Joel's Explorer was just a red blur moving out onto the highway. He rubbed his eyes, and the lids felt as though they were moving over sand.

He'd had a rough night, all right. After work he'd taken a quick shower and put on some fresh clothes, thinking that maybe he and Marla might ride into town to see a movie. But as soon as dinner was over and Derek was cloistered in his room with his computer, Marla started riding his ass. She flung a crumpled piece of paper at him, which turned out to be Missy's phone number. "Who the hell is Missy?" she spat at him.

"Just a customer," he told her. "I was doing an upgrade at Hidden Oaks Apartments. She saw me working and wanted to know some prices. I told her I'd have the office call her back. I forgot to give Rhonda the note."

She watched him, her eyes narrowed. "Bullshit," she said. "That's bullshit and you know it. Why couldn't she just make a call herself?"

He could feel the first flares of anger licking his cheeks. "How the hell should I know? I just told her I'd have somebody call her back."

Marla's lips had pursed so tightly they were almost invisible. "You're lyin'. You're fuckin' lyin' to me."

His hand flew out with a sudden rush of rage. The flat of his palm connected with her cheek with a loud smack, and she went sprawling against the kitchen counter. Grabbing her by the hair on the top of the head, he jerked her face up toward his. Blood trickled from the corner of her mouth, and her eyes were clenched tight as she braced herself for whatever was to come. "Listen to me," he said. "Don't you ever, ever talk to me like that again. Understand?"

She nodded with considerable effort, and the first few tears squeezed from the corners of her eyes.

"Whatever I do outside this house is *my* business. My business. If I want to go rent fifty whores for a fuckin' hour at the Ramada, I'll do it. You *do not* tell me what to do. Is that clear?"

She nodded again, her cheeks glistening with tears, her lips smeared with blood.

Wade gave her hair one last violent tug before pushing her away. "You are so goddamn paranoid. Every time I look at another woman, you think I'm fuckin' her. Well, maybe I am. If you'd spread your legs once in a while I wouldn't have to." He grabbed his keys off the hook by the door and stomped out toward his truck. He'd had enough of her bullshit for one night.

He drove into town to the Wild Horse and was soon parked at the bar with a cold Bud in front of him. And soon he'd had four more. The crowd was wild, the music was too loud, and all the women were either ugly or with somebody. A couple of guys that he recognized, regulars here like himself, nodded to him from a corner booth, but he was in no mood for conversation. His head had begun to ache, and he just wanted to be alone, to let the beer take the edge off everything.

A little while later, standing in the men's room, taking a gusher of a piss, he felt something in his pocket and realized he still had the note with Missy's phone number. A rush of excitement surged through him, and his cock began to stiffen in spite of the beer.

In a little alcove outside the restrooms, he pulled out his phone and punched in her number. After three rings she answered, and her voice sent a buzz of electricity through his gut. "Missy?"

"Yeah, who's this?"

"Hey, it's Wade. Wade Roberts. I met you by the pool yesterday. Cable guy."

"What do you want?"

"Thought I might come by and see you. Take you up on that swim."

She let out a sigh. "Do you know what time it is?"

He glanced at his watch. It was past eleven. "Jesus, I'm sorry. I just lost track of time. You weren't in bed, were you?"

"As a matter of fact, I was."

"I'm sorry," he said again. "Look, if it's too late—"

"I got a call from your wife today."

His body suddenly froze. Marla never said she'd *called* the number. "What?"

"Yeah, so don't ever bother me again. I don't have time to waste on losers like you."

"Missy, wait." But he was talking to a dead line; she had hung up. He shoved the phone back in his pocket. Fucking cunt. He thought briefly of driving over to the apartments anyway, but that was nuts. He wasn't sure which place was hers; hell, he didn't even know her last name.

He threw some bills out on the bar for his tab, not

sure if it was even enough, and stormed out to the parking lot. Even out here, the pulse of the music throbbed in his head. He slid into the truck, started the engine, and pulled out on the street. He didn't know or care where he was headed.

After about an hour of cruising up and down the quiet residential streets, his headache had eased and he turned back toward town, back toward the college campus. As he got closer to the college hangouts, which were noticeably dead this time of the year, one of the places caught his eye. The Capitol, which had once been a movie theater years ago, was now a bar and dance club. Unlike most of the other places on the street, the Capitol seemed to be doing a booming business. He wheeled into the lot and parked between a Nissan and an Oldsmobile, both of which sported Greek window decals.

He hadn't been here since he was a kid, since it still showed movies, and he thought that this was the place he'd come to see a bad horror flick called *Amityville Dollhouse*. The old ticket booth held a mannequin, but a live burly black guy at the door was more than happy to take Wade's five-dollar cover charge.

Inside, the old concession stand was now the bar, and where the auditorium had been was a huge dance floor full of people writhing and dancing beneath pulsing, multi-colored lights. The music blasting over the sound system was some kind of techno dance shit, its repetitive beat thumping at such a breakneck pace that it was impossible to tell whether the music was driving the dancers or the dancers were driving the music.

Most of the crowd seemed to be college age, though he was sure hardly any of them were actually students. The pounding bass of the music coupled with the energy of the crowd around him was suddenly exciting, and the buzz of arousal began to hum through his body.

He got a beer from the bar and moved through the people, looking for somewhere to sit and watch everything.   This place was sure a far cry from the atmosphere of the Wild Horse.   Women were everywhere, many without men and most of them worth a second look; they were young and lively, not the broken-down old crones that frequented the Wild Horse. This was more like Derek's kind of place, and he wondered briefly if the kid had ever tried to get in.

In a far corner, he found a tiny table and took a seat, his gaze drifting across the dance floor.   Strobe lights were flashing monotonously, turning the whole place into a huge pixilated orgy.   Groups of people were dancing together, not just couples; they bounced and gyrated like an undulating human sea under a storm of light.   He leaned against the wall, sipping his beer and watching.

A group of girls were dancing frenetically about ten feet away; a couple of them caught his eye and smiled. He smiled back, flashing his killer grin.   One of them, a blonde, leaned close to the brunette beside her and said something into her ear; it must have been hysterical, because they both burst out laughing.   The blonde looked at him again, and waved him over.   He shook his head, but she waved more insistently, and he reluctantly set down his beer and made his way out onto the floor.

"What's your name?" the blonde asked, not stopping her pace.

"Wade." He was practically screaming to be heard above the music.

"I'm Shelley," she said. She motioned to the brunette. "This is Abby."

Abby smiled at him from beneath her dark, kinky curls. "Hey."

Somehow, the three of them maneuvered into their own frenzied, surging triangle that seemed to take on an energy of its own. And just when he thought he couldn't keep up the pace any longer, when sweat was pouring down his face in rivers, Shelley pressed two tablets into his hand. He looked down at them curiously. At first he thought they were some kind of candy; they were mint green and embossed with a picture of a leaping dolphin. "What are they?" he yelled above the noise.

She laughed breathlessly. "Just take 'em. It's all right."

He popped them into his mouth and felt them dissolve on his tongue into a bitter, chalky paste, which he washed down with a swallow of beer.

After that, everything became fuzzy and strange.

He continued dancing with the girls, and was beginning to think he wasn't doing half bad, when the music just became *part of him* somehow. It was an *extension* of him, flowing through the room and through his body at the same time, a type of radical energy storm. He'd seen those glass globes with sizzling bolts of purple light inside that would follow your fingertips along the surface, and this was almost like that. Except now he was the center of the globe, and his energy, his *light*, seemed connected to everyone else in the room. He could almost see it, like a shimmering, pulsating web extending from his center outward.

Shelley was watching him, smiling. "How ya feel?"

He nodded. "Fantastic."

She grinned wider. "You keep laughing."

"I do?"

"Isn't it great?" Abby said.

Abby's slender body seemed to move in slow motion, writhing with the beat. He wondered what she looked like naked, and then it seemed as though he could see through her clothes, watching her breasts sway, her sleek flat stomach undulate.

Suddenly, he wanted her. He wanted Shelley, too. He wanted both of them, and they wanted him. The three of them were pressed together, moving together with the music, their arms wrapped around each other, and he was kissing them both. He was hard as a stone.

How or when they left the Capitol he could not recall. The next thing he remembered was rolling around in a bed between the two of them. They were all three kissing, licking, moving, flowing. He tasted one, then the other, and he didn't know which. The three of them were one huge writhing, sweating, slippery, fucking mass. He was deep inside Shelley, thrusting powerfully, then he withdrew and plunged into Abby. Something, either a dildo or a vibrator, slipped inside him and began moving in and out. *Really pushing the old envelope now*, he thought. And suddenly he was coming, an orgasm that erupted from his very soul. White sparks of light flashed before him, and then he drifted away to a plane where the pleasure was so painfully intense that his mind could not fathom it. His whole being, even his *skin* was caught up in it; each hair on his body seemed to be firing off its own explosive synapse.

And then in the next instant he was in the truck, heading out of town in the pre-dawn darkness. He was completely naked, and the gas pedal was strange and foreign beneath his bare foot. His heart was pounding—no, *hammering*—in his chest. Sweat was pouring down his face, his back, his stomach. How did he get here? Where were his clothes? The clock on the bank sign said it was a little after four; where in the hell had he been the past few hours? Had he and the girls fallen asleep? Why couldn't he remember?

He realized he was almost home. He managed to pull into the driveway and stop the truck. He killed the ignition and sat there in the dark for a moment. His heart felt like it would burst out of him any second. He took a few deep breaths, trying to calm himself down, but it seemed futile.

Then he remembered those little green tablets. The ones with the dolphins on them. What the hell had they been? It was both wonderful and terrifying at the same time. If Shelley had told him what they were, he couldn't remember. He just knew they had knocked him flat on his ass and he had lost complete control of everything, including his memory.

He took a few more deep breaths, then crawled out of the truck. The house was dark, and he wondered briefly if he should wake Marla to take him to the emergency room.

He let himself in the back door and felt his way through the pitch black to the bedroom. Marla was sleeping, her breathing heavy and steady. Suddenly, he was afraid. What if he died right here on the floor next to the bed?

It's just that his heart was racing. On and on. Why wouldn't it stop? What was in those pills? Were they some kind of uppers? Maybe he needed a sedative, something to counteract it.

He pulled on a pair of shorts from the bureau and quietly made his way back outside to the barn. He switched on the lights, and the sudden brightness stabbed painfully into his head, blinding him momentarily. As his eyes adjusted, he squinted at the tarp-covered Mustang, remembering he had promised Derek they would work on it this weekend. Fuck that, he thought.

Behind his workbench in a little niche of the barn wall was an old cigar box. Inside the box was a small plastic bag of pot, some cigarette papers, a roach clip, and a lighter. His hands were shaking so badly he could hardly roll a joint. He didn't know if this was safe to do on top of those pills or not, but he had to bring himself down, and he had to do it fast.

He turned the lights out and melted back into an old wooden desk chair in the dark, sucking down the sweet smoke and holding it in. Even the pot seemed intensified. What the hell had those pills been?

Gradually, his pounding heart began to slow and he began to cool off. The rivers of sweat dried up, and his mind no longer felt disjointed.

He realized he was exhausted, completely and utterly drained. He went back to the house and crawled between the sheets next to Marla. He was asleep in seconds.

When he awoke, the bedroom was full of light. The clock said it was almost noon, and he could hear Marla stirring around, doing her Saturday cleaning. He sat up on the edge of the bed, his head thick and groggy, his stomach half-nauseated.

In the kitchen, he grabbed a beer from the refrigerator and headed for the front porch. He brushed past Marla, who was wiping down the counters, but didn't say a word. Neither did she; he figured she knew better.

He sat down on the cold concrete of the edge of the porch, his feet dangling, which is where he was when Joel pulled up. He wondered again about his crazy night. Where all did he go and what did he do during those hours between screwing around with Shelley and Abby and waking up naked behind the wheel? It was frightening, and it made him angry.

Beside him, his beer had grown warm and yeasty in the midday sun; he drank it anyway.

1:20 PM

Joel weaved his cart through the aisles of Walmart, trying to stay in the edges of the store as far away from activity as possible. He hated public places like this. Occasionally when pressed with other people in a crowd, he accidentally brushed against them, and their thoughts would float through his head like a drifting radio station. Other times another person's smell might simply be enough to trigger a vision or strong feeling, but that was unpredictable.

A couple of years ago he'd gone with Wade, Marla, and Derek to a Civil War battlefield that was now a state park. They'd planned on having a picnic and maybe renting a boat down on the river. But at one point, while poking around the battlefield, they had ended up in the park's museum, a building that had served as a hospital during the skirmish that had occurred there. Everything was fine for a little while; they moved through the exhibits of dusty rifles and minié balls wordlessly and unimpressed. But when they'd reached the room featuring a display of medical equipment, Joel had been unable to go in. The whole feeling of the air had changed. Its sudden heaviness pressed on him and he couldn't breathe. He bolted, running out of the building to the sunlit park. It wasn't as if he'd seen a ghost or anything; it had simply been an overpowering and oppressive sense of fear. Later he learned the room had served as the operating ward, where doctors had amputated the arms and legs of screaming soldiers, most times without an anesthetic. The panic and terror of those few wounded men was so strong that Joel had been able to sense it a hundred and fifty years later.

Most objects or places he encountered never had

much emotion attached to them. That was particularly lucky considering how much time in other people's homes his job required. There came a point when you didn't want to know certain things about people, especially when you were crawling around under their houses or hunkered down on their bedroom floor.

He maneuvered the cart around the end of the aisle, not really looking at anything, just walking and thinking. He stopped. Someone was following him. He could feel eyes boring into him like drill bits. He froze. He had entered the crafts section, and now he scanned the shelves, pretending to be extremely interested in the colors of yarn, but watching along the periphery of his vision.

And suddenly, there she was. A slender dark-skinned woman in jeans and a red T-shirt. Her black hair was pulled back neatly into plaits, and a slight smile curled the corners of her full lips. She was staring at him with an air of familiarity as if expecting him to greet her. He glanced around and saw that no one else was near.

His first thought was that she was some kind of psycho. But as he looked closer, he knew that could not be the case. She was dressed too neatly, was too clean, and had an aura of wealth about her. But yet, there was something in the back of his mind, something both comfortable and thrilling at the same time, something that made the hairs on the back of his neck prickle. Was he supposed to recognize her? Had she been a customer?

He cleared his throat. "Do I... do I know you?"

She smiled fully, and it was a smile of kindness. "I don't think so," she answered, and her voice was like warm, dripping honey.

"You seem so familiar."

She nodded, still smiling. "You're a sensitive, aren't you?"

His arms and legs went numb. He stared at her blankly. "What?"

"A sensitive. A seer. Whatever you call it. You can read people, can't you?"

He continued to stare, and he felt himself nod almost involuntarily. "How...?

She laughed. "I'm one, too."

A dry laugh of incredulity escaped from his throat. "You're kidding."

"I've been watching you for several weeks." A stab of alarm shot through him; it must have shown on his face, because she laughed again. "I don't mean I've been stalking you or anything. I've just seen you out places, noticed things about you. Watched how you stayed on the fringes of things. Tried not to touch people. That kind of stuff. I wasn't sure at first; I have been wrong before about people. But when I ran into you today, I knew."

"How?"

"I was behind you when you came into the store. I saw the greeter try to give you a cart, but as soon as you touched it, you asked for another one."

All he could do for a moment was blink. It was true; he *had* refused to take that first cart. It had felt *corrupted* somehow, like grabbing hold of—

"It was like grabbing hold of a live wriggling snake," she said, finishing his thought, and laughing at his expression. "I know. I didn't take it, either."

He was smiling in spite of himself. "What do you think it was?"

She shook her head. "Not sure. Maybe the person who'd used it before was psychotic. Who knows?"

He was beginning to feel as though he had passed over into a surreal dream. This beautiful black woman had appeared from nowhere knowing bizarre, intimate aspects of his life. She was practically reading his mind. Unease again overtook him. "Look," he said, "I don't mean to be rude. You seem like a very nice person. I'm just not interested in anyone right now."

A burst of laughter popped out of her, and she covered her mouth. "I'm sorry," she said, stifling her giggles. "I didn't mean for you to think I was hitting on you. It did sound like that, didn't it?"

He was more confused than ever. His face was suddenly hot and flushed. "Then what do you want?"

She was laughing, shaking her head, showing her perfect white teeth. She dug into her purse and pulled out a notepad. "My name's Deb," she said. "There are about fifteen of us now. We meet one Sunday afternoon a month over in Springfield at St. Thomas Church. Tomorrow's the day. Two o'clock." She scribbled this information down and handed him the note.

He shook his head, bewildered. "I don't understand."

She looked at him directly. "We're like you. All of

us."

"All fifteen of you?"

"Well, some of us have different gifts, but it basically amounts to the same thing."

He stared at the paper in his hand, then back at Deb. "I'm sorry," he said. "I'm just a little flustered."

She laughed. "I understand. You thought you were the only one, didn't you?"

"Well, no, not exactly. I mean, I always *assumed* there were others. I just didn't expect so many. So close."

"We're not all from Springfield or Cedar Hill," Deb said. "Some of the members drive a couple of hours to get to the meetings."

"Really?"

She nodded, then turned to look back at her half-filled cart. "Well, I should really be going. I hope you'll join us. If not tomorrow, then another time."

"What exactly do you do at these meetings?" He was beginning to feel a touch of skepticism, and he worked to keep it out of his voice.

"It's more of a support group than anything," she said. "It's just a place to belong. To make new friends."

He shrugged, still noncommittal. "I'll think about it."

"Most of us have spent our lives either denying we had the gift or feeling like freaks. At our meetings we can feel normal."

Normal. He liked the sound of that. He had never at any point in his life felt normal. He glanced at the note again.

She smiled and grabbed her cart. "I really do hope you'll come. Once you meet everyone, you'll know you don't have to be alone anymore." She started moving away. "Goodbye, Joel."

He stood silently, watching her go. He realized that at no time during their conversation had he given her his name.

5:42 PM

Halloran had finally decided he could stomach the Mexican leftovers, but now they had been in the refrigerator so long they had started to mold. He scraped them off into the trash and let the plate clatter into the sink. Mel sat on the counter, watching him intently. "So much for dinner," Halloran said. There was nothing else to eat in the apartment, so now he supposed he would have to head out. "Guess it's Mickey D's tonight," he told the cat.

His phone rang, and he flopped down on the sofa and answered it.

"Halloran?" It was Pettus. "I need you to come down here to the station if you can."

"Now?"

"Are you in the middle of something?"

"Not really. Just gonna go grab a bite to eat."

Pettus grunted. "Well, get it to go."

"What's up?"

"You're gonna love this. We got another missing kid."

Halloran's heart sank. "Another one?"

"Yep. Another girl."

"I'll be right there."

* * *

Her name was Carmelita Santos. Her parents, both migratory workers from Mexico, were already seated in his office talking to Chapman when he arrived. The mother wept softly against her husband's shoulder, her round, brown cheeks glistening with tears. Mr. Santos sat slumped over, his dark eyes glassy and fearful beneath the red brim of his St. Louis Cardinals cap.

Chapman was scribbling information onto a report form, a chewed-up Bic pen clamped in his fingers. "Carmelita is how old?" he asked.

"*Quince años*," said Mr. Santos, then shook his head, seemingly embarrassed that he had lapsed into Spanish. "*Soy arrepentido*. Fifteen years."

Chapman noted it on his report. "Tell us again what happened."

Mr. Santos's eyes flashed hotly. "We have already told everyone. Three times."

Chapman smiled sympathetically. "I know. But let's go over it one more time." He nodded toward Halloran. "Lieutenant Halloran and I will be investigating your daughter's disappearance. I'd just like him to hear everything from you."

The Santoses eyed Halloran suspiciously. "You will find our Carmelita?" Mrs. Santos asked.

"We're certainly going to try," Halloran told her.

They spoke hesitantly at first but gradually opened up and began talking faster, at times in Spanish and then repeating themselves in English. The three of them were living in a rooming house on Bellevue Road, an area on the fringes of town where most of the migrants stayed during farming season. Carmelita had left just after lunch to meet some friends at the city park. The friends returned about two o'clock. Carmelita was not with them; they had not seen her all day. Somewhere in the four blocks between the rooming house and the park, she had vanished. The Santoses and the others staying at the house had searched the neighborhood for two hours, but they found nothing.

Halloran pulled a chair into the office from the hallway. "You know of any reason why your daughter would run away?"

The Santoses shook their heads adamantly.

"Any problems with boys? Or drugs?"

Mr. Santos looked at Halloran, his face hard. "Our Carmelita was happy," he said.

Mrs. Santos pulled a photograph from her shirt pocket and handed it over to Halloran. It was a slightly fuzzy snapshot of a beautiful slender girl who looked just on the verge of womanhood. She was smiling into the camera showing the dimples at the corners of her mouth. Her hair, long and black, was tucked playfully behind her ears. She was wearing an ash-gray jersey with purple sleeves and blue jeans.

"She says Carmelita was wearing that shirt today," Chapman said.

"*Por favor*," whispered Mrs. Santos, tears streaming down her cheeks. "*Mi bebé. Mi bebé.*"

Halloran looked at her and nodded. "*Entiendo.*"

10:55 PM

Joel sat in the recliner, staring at the television. *Saturday Night Live* was on the screen, but he wasn't watching it. Beside him on the end table a cigarette sat in the ashtray; its length had smoldered to gray ash until the fire had hit the filter and it sputtered itself out.

In his fingers was the note Deb had given him today. He had tried to tell himself all evening that it had just been a chance encounter—a fluke. That she was like some psychic Hare Krishna handing out Post-It note equivalents of flowers. But he knew otherwise. She had sought him out. And she had been telling the truth. He was sure of it.

And she had known his name. He shuddered with a sudden chill.

A place to belong. That's what she had said. And he wanted that. Needed it.

Maybe he would go tomorrow. Just to check it out. He didn't have to stay long. And no one said he ever had to go back if he didn't like it.

He could try it. Just once.

SUNDAY, JULY 8

11:30 AM

Marla sat in the pew of the church, holding her open bible and watching the minister but thinking of Wade.

Yesterday he had staggered to bed at five in the morning, reeking of pot and sex. She pretended to be asleep until she heard him snoring, then she sat up in bed, staring out at the early gray dawn as her eyes brimmed with tears.

She wondered where he had been and with whom, although it probably didn't make much difference. She looked down at his head of dark curls, his tanned shoulders, his muscled arm ringed with the tribal tattoo peeking just above the sheets. She tried to remember how it felt to love him, how she had felt when they were younger and she would hang on to him for all she was worth when he made love to her, pulling him as deep inside as she could. But now all she could feel was a painful loathing.

Why did he stay? What good was it possibly doing for him to hang around? Maybe he simply enjoyed the sadistic kick of making her miserable, of hurting her, of making her feel like a caged animal. Maybe that was it.

She had dragged herself out of bed and made her way to the kitchen, where she sat at the table in her T-shirt and panties while the coffee brewed. She had noticed his clothes were not in the floor where he usually dropped them when he crawled into bed, and she thought that odd; then she wondered if he had hidden them from her. But why would he? He didn't care if she knew he was out with other women (he most assuredly had been), and he didn't care if there were telltale signs somewhere on his clothes (there probably were). What was worse was that she didn't care either. So why would he hide them from her? She had thought about asking him when he got up just before lunchtime, but when he stumbled through the kitchen to the porch, he looked like walking death, and she thought it wise to simply ignore him.

After Joel stopped by, Wade had come back in and cleaned up. "I'm goin' into town," he told her. He climbed into his truck and barreled out of the driveway, his rear tires spitting gravel. She had not seen him since.

This morning when he was still not home, she started to call the police because he might have had an accident of some kind. But she didn't. It was, after all, not the first time he had disappeared only to return later with no explanation. He was like a tomcat out searching for a female in heat. It made her sick. But she did not want to worry about it because that was what he wanted her to do. She knew he hoped she had been awake all night waiting for him, expecting him to call and say he was in trouble. Or worse, for the state highway patrol to show up on her doorstep with bad news.

Instead, she called Joel. She only meant to ask if he had seen Wade, but instead she found herself sobbing over the phone and telling him that his brother had been out God-knew-where for the past two nights, and that she had no idea who he had been with or what he had been up to. And Joel had been angry; he hadn't said so, but she could hear it in his voice. He told her not to worry, that Wade was probably all right, that the two of them would have a chat, and for her to call as soon as she heard anything. She hung up feeling more than a little embarrassed, and somewhat fearful that Wade would be furious with her for calling Joel.

It wasn't fair. If Wade didn't give a damn about her, he should at least think of Derek. A boy needed to have his father around.

She looked over at him now, sitting complacently next to her in his crisp white shirt and khakis. There were times when she worried dreadfully over him. She smiled at him, and he caught her eye and smiled back. He really was a handsome boy, she thought. He had his father's dark curly hair and her dark eyes. He was a looker already.

"A-*men!*" shouted the man behind her, making her jump. Derek looked at her. Some of the teenage girls in the back had seen her and they snickered. *Damn them*, she thought. *Damn them to hell.*

When the service was over and she and Derek filed out of the church with the others, Marla did her best to keep up the chitchat with those around her. *Yes, I'm fine. How're you? How's that grandson of yours? Your kids enjoying their summer off from school? Still like your job? Sure has been hot.*

She wondered about these other women in the congregation. Did any of these women have to live with what she did? Did any of them have to pretend everything was just grand when it was really black and rotten inside?

Sally and Rob Carpenter floated by in their new Buick Regal like a dream. Sally waved to her, like Queen Elizabeth in a horse-drawn coach. Rob owned an appliance store in town and Sally taught fifth grade. She tried to imagine them in bed. Sally on her hands and knees, her hair all disheveled and hanging in her face; Rob behind her, pumping away, sweat pouring down his face, chest and arms, his thinning hair splayed across his damp forehead. *Let's push the envelope tonight, Sal.* She shuddered.

"Mom?" Derek said, and she looked at him. "I was talking to you."

She smiled distractedly and slid on her sunglasses. "I'm sorry, what?"

"I said, can we go to Pizza Hut? I'm starving."

She unlocked the car door. "Not today, babe."

* * *

When they pulled into the driveway, she was half-relieved, half-disappointed to see Wade's truck there. Wade was reclining on the front porch in one of the plastic lawn chairs, still wearing the clothes he had left in yesterday. His shirt was wrinkled and damp and clung to him like fungus. He took a drag off his cigarette, watching them get out of the car.

"Dad!" shouted Derek, crossing the lawn to the porch. "Can we work on the car today? Please?"

"I don't know," said Wade. "I'm pretty tired."

Marla glared at him as she came up the steps. "Hey," she said.

He nodded at her. "Hey."

And now that she was close to him, he reeked of beer and sweat. Fury swept over her. "Out kinda late, huh?" she said before she could stop herself.

Wade's eyes were red-rimmed and tired, but she still caught a flash of anger. "Yeah, I guess I was."

She brushed past him into the coolness of the house, leaving the two of them on the porch. *Just pushing the envelope*, she thought.

1:35 PM

He had left early because he wasn't sure how long it would take him to find the church. He didn't have a need to go to Springfield often, and though he knew where most of the major streets and landmarks were, he wasn't familiar with St. Thomas Church. He spotted it, though, as soon as he entered the city. It was a large rambling brick structure with an open bell tower and stained glass windows. He'd seen it before, but he supposed he'd never paid any attention to it.

He was thirty minutes early, so he drove around a nearby McDonald's and got a Coke. He sat in the parking lot of the restaurant sipping his drink and looking at St. Thomas' bell tower above the treetops. He was nervous. His heart pounded in the pit of his stomach, like he was a teenager on a first date. He wasn't sure what to expect. What would these people be like? How weird would they be? What kind of meetings did they hold? He pictured strange rituals where everyone wore dark robes and chanted, or where they all cavorted naked in a circle.

He finally drove over to the church, circling around it, looking for signs of life. Behind the church proper was a new aluminum building with a sign out front that said "ACTIVITY CENTER." There were several cars parked in the lot. This must be the place.

He parked his Explorer as close to the street as he could, took a last-second glance at his face in the rear-view mirror, and headed out across the hot asphalt toward the building, his heart knocking a mile a minute. There were no windows in the building, and the glass on the front door was tinted, so he couldn't see inside. Were they watching him now? Watching him trudging across the parking lot, sweating like some massive, frightened beast? He took a breath, grabbed the door and opened it.

A blast of refreshingly cool air hit him at once, and at first he thought he was mistaken, that he had walked into a bridge party or a bridal shower. The large, open room was well lit and clean and smelled of the fresh flowers decorating a buffet line full of snacks. Several people milled about, talking with one another and eating off paper plates, some sitting at small round tables. One of the men, Joel was startled to see, was a priest. Everyone looked so ordinary. Surely this wasn't right. He turned to go before anyone spotted him.

"Joel!"

He looked back and saw Deb coming toward him, smiling broadly, and he felt a self-conscious grin appear on his face. "Hi."

"You came," she said, clearly pleased.

He nodded. "Thought I might check it out."

"Not what you expected is it?"

He laughed, shaking his head. "No. I thought..." He stopped, not sure how to finish.

Deb was nodding. "I know," she said, and he truly believed she did. She motioned him toward the others. "Come on, let me introduce you to some folks." He followed her toward the murmuring group, and nearly jumped a foot when she clapped her hands and said loudly, "All right, everyone, your attention, please." They were all looking at him now, he noticed, but not in puzzlement; they seemed to already know why he was there. "Everyone, I'd like you to meet Joel. He's the one I told you about."

They all greeted him, and Deb introduced them one by one in a flurry of names and faces he knew he would never remember. There was a young blonde girl who appeared to be in her late teens, and an old gentleman who looked at least eighty; everyone else fit somewhere in between, and seemed to come from all ethnic backgrounds and social circles. Deb introduced the priest last, a distinguished looking pudgy man with thick gray hair and blue eyes. "This is Father Michael. He's not a sensitive himself, but he lets us use the church's facilities for our meetings."

Father Michael nodded to him. "Good to meet you, Joel. I think you'll find everyone here is friendly and accommodating."

Gradually, everyone drifted back into their own conversations, and Joel moved to take a seat at the table next to Father Michael. "So how did a priest get involved in something like this?" he said.

Father Michael smiled. "Deb's one of my flock," he said. "I've known of her gift for years, knew her struggle with accepting it. When she found a few others like herself, I encouraged her to start a group. They met at her house at first, but as more and more people became involved, she knew she had to have a larger place. I told her to feel free to use the church's activity center."

"That was nice."

Father Michael shrugged. "Whole purpose of having the place."

"So do you come here just to keep an eye on things or what?"

"I have a real interest in it, in what the old-timers call 'second sight.' I believe that it truly is a gift, though I understand the people who have it would tend to disagree."

"Yeah," Joel said. "Myself included."

"Now, you take Joseph over there," Father Michael said, pointing toward the old man Joel had noticed earlier. "When he was a young man, his family was convinced he was a demon. Or that he'd been touched by Satan. They were scared to death of him. Especially after…" The priest looked away.

"What?"

Father Michael looked back at him abruptly. "Did you ever hear of the big train disaster here in Springfield? Happened in 'twenty-five or 'twenty six."

Joel nodded. Everyone knew that story. How a locomotive had jumped the track one sunny April morning and plowed right through Springfield Elementary School, completely demolishing the building. No one had even been scratched; all the students and teachers had gone to the town common for a picnic that day and the school had been empty.

"Joseph had organized the picnic downtown," said Father Michael. "He knew something was going to happen that day. Saw it in a dream."

"Really?" Joel looked at the man now, just a frail, little man dressed in a natty sports jacket and droopy trousers.

"I'm convinced," the priest continued, "that God used Joseph's ability that day to save those people."

Joel stared at the wall, thinking about the train that had snuffed out the lives of his mother and stepfather. If he had known, if he could have seen, would he have warned them? Would he have kept them alive, even though it would have meant who knew how many more years of violent abuse from Clifton? He didn't know; it was just a dead end question. Like what would have happened had the school been full. "What's the point?"

he said.

Father Michael looked at him. "Excuse me?"

"What was the point of giving Joseph a vision, of making him responsible?"

"I'm not sure what you mean."

"If God could do that, then why not just keep the train from derailing in the first place? Why not just make it easy?

Father Michael smiled crookedly, looking away. "It's not our purpose to question God," he said. "Perhaps it was a test."

"A test? For who?"

"For Joseph."

Joel glanced at the others, and his gaze fell on the young blonde girl. She was talking animatedly to Deb, holding a cookie in one hand and a Diet Coke in the other. "Who's the kid?" he asked.

Father Michael smiled. "That's Dana West," he said. "She's only been aware of her gift a couple of years, but Deb says she's exceptionally strong."

"How old is she?"

"Older than she looks. Twenty-one." Father Michael pointed to a nondescript couple sitting nearby. "That's her parents there. Frank and Bonnie."

"So they…?"

"Yes. The whole family."

Joel looked at the three of them, incredulous. "This kind of thing tends to run in families, doesn't it?"

"So I've been told. It sometimes skips a generation or two, but it's not rare that parents and children share it." Father Michael took a sip from his foam cup.

"They live in your neck of the woods, by the way."

"Cedar Hill?"

"Yep. Dana attends the college there."

Joel glanced around and caught a red-bearded guy looking at him. The other man quickly turned his attention to the floor. Something about him gave Joel the creeps.

Father Michael followed Joel's line of vision. "Barry's had a very troubled life. Tried to commit suicide. Bounced around from job to job, city to city. This is the first place he's ever felt comfortable with himself and his ability." He looked at Joel. "I hope you'll feel comfortable here, too, Joel."

* * *

A little while later, the group gathered the folding metal chairs into a circle, and they all sat facing the center. Deb led the group as they discussed the various events of their lives the past month. Most talked of their feelings of self-doubt and guilt, of their loathing for their abilities. Some, he was surprised to discover, regularly used drugs in an effort to deaden their feelings, to "desensitize" themselves. A few, including Barry, spoke of past suicide attempts. All, however, seemed open and honest; no one appeared to be lying or secretive. Joel had never been to a meeting of Alcoholics Anonymous, but this is how imagined one would be.

Finally, Deb turned to him. "So, Joel, what do you think? Are we all crazy?"

Everyone laughed, and Joel smiled. "You're all nuts," he said, and they laughed louder.

6:45 PM

Halloran sat in his office, sipping stale black coffee from a foam cup, letting his thoughts drift in the quiet. There had been no sign of Carmelita Santos.

A massive search party organized of people from the neighborhood, the police, and other volunteers had meticulously combed through the park and surrounding streets, looking everywhere. They searched behind every building, in every ravine, under every bush. Nothing. Carmelita had vanished without a trace. Finally, in the middle of the afternoon, a canine unit was brought in from Springfield; that, too, failed to turn up any clues.

Mr. and Mrs. Santos were nearly incapacitated with grief and worry. Now, more than yesterday, they eyed Halloran and Chapman with suspicion, as if the police were somehow to blame for their daughter's disappearance. It was understandable, but these days Halloran found it harder not to take such things personally.

Chapman stuck his head in the door. "Hey."

Halloran sat up. "Hey yourself. Come on in."

Chapman flopped his lanky frame into one of the chairs opposite Halloran. "Don't guess there's anything new."

Halloran shook his head. He held up his cup. "Want some coffee? I think it's only about eight hours old."

Chapman gave a strained laugh. "No, thanks." He rubbed his eyes. "Long day."

"No kidding."

He looked at Halloran. "You think these two cases

are related? Sarah Jo and Carmelita?"

Halloran took a swig of coffee. "I'd bet money on it. Same circumstances. Both girls about the same age."

Chapman licked his lips. "I think we've got a serial offender."

Halloran nodded grimly. "I agree."

"What do you think our chances are of finding the Santos girl alive?"

Halloran stared at the wall. He drained his cup and plopped it onto the desk. "Between you and me, almost none."

10:47 PM

Wade lay beside Marla, listening to her steady breathing and staring up into the nothingness of the dark room. Boy, he had really been fucked up yesterday. He barely remembered getting up. Barely remembered Joel pulling in and talking to him. Barely remembered getting dressed and heading back into town. All he could recall clearly was sitting at the Wild Horse later with a beer and a plate of cheese-drenched potato skins, listening to some old geezer next to him ramble on drunkenly about his dog.

When he was finally feeling alive again, he left the bar and drove across town to the cable office. He was still tired. God, was he tired. In the lounge of the office was a large sofa, and he stretched out on it and slept for a few hours.

He awoke slightly achy but clear-headed a little after eight o'clock. He splashed some water on his face and ran a wet hand through his hair. Straightened the collar of his shirt. Refreshed, he headed back out to the truck and took off toward the other side of town.

The Capitol was already bustling, even at this early hour. Once inside, he scoured the dancing mob for Shelley and Abby, and when he didn't see them, he grabbed a table and watched the dance floor, nursing a beer and filling up the ashtray. The crowd was about the same tonight—lots of attractive women, all young and lithe, but no one he felt he could connect with.

After an hour, just when he thought he couldn't take the boredom any longer, he felt a hand on his shoulder. Shelley and Abby had appeared behind him. Seeing them again immediately charged his system, and the three of them were soon on the floor with everyone else. Shelley produced more of her magical tablets, and again he felt that wonderful, beautiful connection to everyone and everything. This time, however, he was prepared for it, and the feeling wasn't quite as intense.

For the second night in a row, the three of them ended up in the same bed together. It was an apartment that Shelley and Abby shared, he discovered, but he never could quite figure out if the two of them shared the bed when they were alone. Again, the sex was mind-blowing and when he awoke this time, he was at least still in the bed between them, the morning sunlight spilling over the white sheets and their tangled limbs.

He climbed carefully from the bed and pulled on his jeans, lit a cigarette and looked around for his shirt.

"What're you doin'?" said a groggy voice. It was Abby, brushing her tangled curls from her eyes.

"I gotta go," he said.

"It's too early."

"It's after ten."

"Stay and have breakfast."

He slipped on his shirt and stepped into his shoes. "I can't. I really gotta go."

Abby flopped back down. "Your clothes from the other night are on that chair over there."

He found them and tucked them under his arm, then knelt beside her, kissing her twice on the lips. "Give one of those to Shelley for me."

She smiled sleepily. "You're beautiful," she said, and then she was drifting off again.

Outside, the sun was dazzling and blinding as he left town, and when he got to the house, he was relieved to see Marla's car was gone. He tossed his dirty clothes in the laundry room and grabbed a bowl of spaghetti from the refrigerator. He stood at the kitchen sink, staring through the window at the back yard and the barn, slurping down the cold noodles and acrid sauce until the bowl was empty.

He had promised Derek they would work on the Mustang, and he had blown it off yesterday, thinking today would be better. But here he was, dog-ass tired and hung over again, and he knew there was no way he would feel like bending over an engine out in the heat.

He was just like Clifton.

No, he thought. *God, no.*

When Wade was thirteen, puberty had hit him like a brick wall. Seemingly overnight he went from a scrawny little kid to a six-foot teen who had to shave at least twice a week. His hormones had been working overtime; in addition to the occasional wet dreams (which were scary at first, but he grew to look forward to them) and the sudden appearance of hair in all kinds of strange places, Wade was cursed with a severe case of acne. His face and shoulders—even his back and arms—erupted in ugly, angry, red blemishes that sometimes swelled to the size of boils. He tried everything to rid himself of them—soaps, lotions, ointments. Nothing seemed to help. If he had known then that in a year or so the condition would suddenly disappear, almost like magic, it might not have been so unbearable. The physical pain was bad enough, but the torment of going to school with his appearance was pure hell.

One day while he was standing in line in the lunchroom some ass-wipe two years his senior made the mistake of calling him "leper," apparently trying to coin a new nickname. Wade jumped on him and beat the shit out of him, breaking a lunch tray over the fucker's head in the process. He had been suspended for three days over the incident, but no one had made fun of him again. Ever.

Unfortunately, Clifton was out of work at the time, and he spent his days getting drunk and railing against everything he didn't agree with. Though he especially hated the government and taxes, he wasn't above going off on a tangent when the occasion called for it. When Wade was sent home, Clifton demanded an explanation. Wade gave it to him—told him what the guy had said to him, what he had called him, and what Wade had done to him. For an instant, Clifton's eyes were clear and lucid; the next moment they were drunk and hazy. "You know what causes them pimples," Clifton told him. "It's because you play with yourself too god-damned much.   You leave your cock alone, them things'll go away."

Infuriated, Wade stormed off to his room, not only insulted and offended by Clifton's remarks but wounded by his lack of understanding and sympathy.   He flopped on his bed, his eyes stinging with angry, hurt tears.   In a little while, drained by everything that had happened, he fell asleep.

He was awakened abruptly by his door being flung open.   Clifton stood just outside his room, swaying slightly, a bottle of Jim Beam clutched in his hand. "What're you doin' in here?" he demanded.   He tipped the bottle and drained the last of the bourbon into his gaping mouth.

"Nothin'," Wade answered.   "Sleepin'."

"You're doin' it again, ain'tcha?"

Wade shook his head, trying to clear out the grogginess.   "What?   No.   I was sleepin'.   Honest."   He moved to scuttle off the bed and out of the room, but Clifton was too quick for him.   He seized him by the shirt collar and slammed him facedown onto the bed.   For a drunk, he was surprisingly strong and agile.

"You're gonna see how they do it, the fuckin' faggots.   You're gonna get it like they get it."

Wade felt his jeans being wrenched down, and terror seized him.   He was screaming, hoping his mother—or anyone—could hear him.   Clifton pinned him down and held him tight against the mattress.   "Shut up, faggot," he whispered in Wade's ear, and his breath was like acid. Sweat was pouring down his face, dripping onto the bed. "Let's see how you like it now." From the corner of his eye, Wade could see the lips of the up-turned bottle moving toward his bare buttocks.

With the last of his strength, Wade pushed himself off the bed, flinging Clifton back across the room. The bottle hit the floor and shattered. Clifton slammed into the wall, then slid down to the floor, his eyes round and startled. Wade went for him. "You bastard!" His fist connected with Clifton's nose, and a sudden spray of blood erupted down the man's shirt. "You fucking *bastard!*" Clifton curled into a ball as Wade's fists pummeled him.

There was a sudden gasping, choking sound. Clifton's face was twisted and red and wet, and he was crying. Wade brought his foot back and kicked Clifton as hard as he could in the side.

"I'm sorry, I'm sorry," Clifton kept repeating, his voice broken and sobbing.

"Don't you ever fuckin' touch me again," Wade spat at him.

Wade never told anyone about the incident, not even Joel. He was left feeling violated and ashamed, but he hoped that by fighting back he had cured Clifton of his mean streak.

That lasted about two months. The hostility began at first with a few smacks to the back of Wade's head; soon it had escalated back to point it had been before. Wade remembered the bottle incident, and was tempted to fight Clifton again. But after Clifton punched him and broke his jaw—this time for smoking, the self-righteous prick—Wade was too afraid of him. He made the decision that he would escape from that hell as soon as he got the chance, and when Marla came up pregnant he took the opportunity and ran.

Marla's parents let them move into the abandoned trailer behind their house, and at first Wade was happy. Being away from Mama and Clifton was almost as good as heaven. But after a few months he knew he had made a mistake. Being married was simply another kind of hell. But leaving Marla would have meant going back home, and he sure didn't want that. But gradually he realized there was one critical difference between living with his stepfather and living with Marla: here, Wade was in control. Marla might argue and disagree with him, but she didn't fight back. Not anymore.

He knew she was not happy with him. No more than he was happy with her. In fact, she *hated* him sometimes; he could see it in her eyes. And sometimes he hated her, and there was *pleasure* in hurting her. But he tried not to think of that. Besides, Marla was an adult; no one was stopping her if she wanted to leave.

Now, in the musky darkness of their bedroom, he rolled over to her and put an arm around her waist, settling in to finally go to sleep. Marla dozed on, unaware that a hand she had cowered from so many times now lay gently and almost affectionately across her stomach.

MONDAY, JULY 9

10:17 AM

Joel and Wade were working on a job at Mayor Carver's house in Marvin Heights, a gated subdivision out by the college, and Joel was angry.

Not only had Wade refused to tell him anything about where he had been all weekend, but he became absolutely livid when Joel told him that Marla had called looking for him. Joel knew it was none of his business where Wade had been, and in truth he didn't care. But Wade had a family, and he had responsibilities. And—*dammit*—he had the obligation to tell his wife what the hell he'd been up to all weekend. Joel only pushed so far; Wade had his limits, and they were undeniably short. Reluctantly, Joel tried to focus on his work, which at the moment was adding another cable outlet in the mayor's living room.

The room was huge, and it likely would have swallowed Joel's whole house. One entire wall was lined with shelves crammed with books, and opposite that was a stone fireplace so massive that the mantle was several inches above their heads; on the paneled wall above that was the stuffed head of a large moose, its glass eyes peering down at them in a rather condescending way. A monstrous grand piano sat beside a pair of French doors that looked out over a regal patio and a large pool beyond. The furniture was sparse and tailored, clustered into groups about the room, what Martha Stewart would have undoubtedly called "conversation areas." Joel was more accustomed to conventional surroundings—rooms in which he felt like a colossal floundering whale, afraid to move lest he scrape shelves and tables free of their knick-knacks with his awkward, beefy limbs. The living rooms of old ladies cluttered with dusty framed photographs resting on crocheted doilies or the dens of families where so many toys littered the room that you couldn't walk. Here he felt small. Well, not small exactly, but maybe this was how a normal-sized person felt in a normal-sized room.

Mrs. Carver, a large-boned woman with short blonde hair and thick lips, darted in and out of the room nervously, as if she feared they would take off with the family heirlooms. "I'll be in the kitchen," she told them from the doorway. "If you need me."

Wade finished drilling a hole into the floor and blew the sawdust from it. "Go downstairs to the basement and find the service entrance," he told Joel. "Run a tap from the main cable over to here."

Joel skulked across the great room toward the hall where he had seen Mrs. Carver disappear. "Hello?" he called. The hallway seemed endless, its walls lined with plaques and certificates, testimonies to the mayor's influence.

He stopped and stared at one.

Presented to
MAYOR LARRY CARVER
In appreciation of his years of dedicated service.
Cedar Hill Park Board

Joel wondered what the mayor could have done to receive this plaque, other than show up at the meetings and approve the budget.

There were countless others. The Cedar Hill School Chess Club. The Rotary Club. The Optimists Club. Mayor Carver was indeed a busy man.

There was a photograph of the mayor receiving some type of medal on a blue ribbon from a balding, bespectacled goon Joel recognized from TV as the governor. The mayor towered over him; he was a robust man, tall and muscular beneath his suit, with a finger-combed mop of salt-and-pepper hair and a neatly trimmed beard just starting to go gray. Joel stared at him. He'd never seen him outside of the fuzzy photos in the newspaper or waving distantly from a convertible in the Veterans Day parade. He looked...odd. Handsome and smiling, yet the smile didn't quite reach his eyes. His eyes were soft and brown, but something about them seemed flat and emotionless, almost glassy.

Like the eyes of the moose in the other room. Dead and cold.

"Can I help you?" Joel looked away from the picture to see Mrs. Carver staring at him. She was twisting her diamond wedding band.

"I need to get to the basement," he said.

She nodded and pointed to a plain door at the end of the hall. "Light switch is on your left."

Joel descended into the musty darkness, nearly bashing his forehead against a beam before reaching the landing. The dim bare bulbs hanging from the ceiling lit a pathway through piles of old furniture and moldy cardboard boxes. He pulled the flashlight off his belt and shined it into the dark corners, scaring up a few spiders, searching for the entrance of the cable into the house.

Though his eyes searched the dusty beams above him, his mind was on yesterday. On the group. The sensitives. He wondered what kind of work some of them did. It was difficult to imagine any of them in a factory or teaching school; some of them, like Barry and Joseph he was fairly sure, had no jobs at all.

He headed for the corner of the basement where he thought the cable entrance should be, playing the light at the mass of wires and cables tacked onto the crossbeams. Just as he found it, the toe of his shoe caught against the leg of an old kitchen chair, and the pile of newspaper clippings on its seat spilled into the floor. Spitting out a curse, he knelt and began picking them up.

Then he saw it. Just below a window encrusted with

dust, out of his line of sight when he had been standing, was a break in the drywall where pulsing light was spilling through. There was a door built into the wall; he could see the hinges. Curious, he stepped over to it and felt around until he got a grip on an edge, then pulled it open.

Behind the door was a small room, about eight feet square, no more than a closet, really. Its walls, floor, and ceiling were upholstered in red vinyl. Light came from four strategically placed recessed strobe fixtures that illuminated the only other object in the room: a sort of leather sling that was suspended from above by shiny chrome chains. The strobes pulsed slowly and monotonously, like the flash of some insane phantom photographer.

He stared, dumbfounded. He had an idea, of course, what the sling was for, and a smile played at the corner of his mouth. He tried to picture the mayor's wife strung up in here like a slab of meat, naked and sweating. *Give it to me, Larry!* A dry laugh escaped his lips. Without thinking he brushed his fingertips against the sling.

Instantly a flood of visions and emotions crossed before him and was gone. He reeled a bit, looking at the thing. Then he reached out and grabbed it.

What he saw was a mass of writhing, tangled bodies locked together in sexual bliss beneath the flashing lights. Images swam on top of images, dark indistinguishable faces dissolving from one to another. Voices moaned and screamed—some in pleasure, some in pain, most a combination of both. Once he saw Larry

Carver's face vividly, his features pinched and distorted in ecstasy.

But it was the thrill shooting through him that would not allow him to let go of the sling. The sexual energy pounding in his chest, his loins. He had never felt anything like it. It felt so strong, like a jolt of electricity. Wave after wave flowing through him. An orgasmic spark that began in his groin and spread through his limbs like a shock of lightning. It was sheer, undiluted lust of a magnitude he never knew could exist.

Only the sudden weakness in his legs made him let go, and he steadied himself against the vinyl wall. His breath was heaving, and a viscous sweat had broken out on his forehead. Then he realized something else: he had an erection. The first one he'd had in ten years.

Trembling, he stepped out of the room and shut the wall behind him. He wondered about the faceless, nameless people he had envisioned, some in the sling, some writhing on the floor. He wondered what the governor would have thought of Mayor Larry Carver if he'd been able to see what Joel just experienced. Probably would have strangled him with that blue ribbon. But then, who knew? Maybe the governor had been a guest here. Maybe the governor had even been in the sling. Maybe the governor had liked it.

Joel bent down to grab the newspapers he had scattered over the floor and began stacking them. He stopped. All of the papers had to do with Sarah Jo McElvoy. He looked at a front-page story from April: *Girl Still Missing*. Sarah Jo smiled up at him from the color picture—a school portrait most likely—that accompanied the article, and Joel felt a chill up his spine. The stories started with her disappearance and went right up through finding her body last week. He shuffled through the pile. There were dozens of them, all stories from the Cedar Hill *Post-Dispatch*, from front-page articles to small stories buried farther in the paper.

Suddenly, the red room didn't seem quite so sexy. He began to wonder exactly what had happened in there.

Was the mayor involved in this? Had the mayor taken that girl? If so, what had he done with her? *To* her?

He wondered if he had missed something in those visions, if there was some small part that had gotten by him while he was lost in the flood of ecstasy. But he didn't think so. He could try it again, grab the sling and search his feelings again, but the visions before were so murky—more physical than visual, and nothing really clear except Larry Carver's moaning face.

And besides, now he was afraid. If there *were* something to all this, if the mayor were somehow involved in the girl's death, Joel wasn't sure he wanted to find out this way. Not in a dank, musty basement surrounded by dark shadows and a pulsing strobe light.

He looked again at the clipped articles in his hand, wondering if he should go to the police, doubting that he ever could, knowing he would never be able to convince them of anything. What would he say to them? There was no way he would ever tell them about his ability, and even if he did they would never believe him.

Perhaps he could just tell them about the room, about the articles. Maybe it would throw some suspicion this way. He debated taking a few of the articles to show the police, but then decided against it. Anyone could cut things out of the paper; that certainly didn't make a murderer. But he had to admit it was still strange.

He finished stacking up the newspapers and moved on to his real work, his fingers trembling.

Not surprisingly, his erection was gone.

1:40 PM

Halloran and Chapman stood at the edge of the cemetery with Chief Pettus, watching the mourners file back to their cars from the green tent set presumptuously amid the gray headstones. Today, Sarah Jo McElvoy was finally being laid to rest in Our Lady of Peace Gardens. Halloran got just a glimpse of Sarah Jo's mother; she was wearing dark glasses against the intense summer sun and had a fresh cigarette between her lips. A lady in a navy blue suit—who was probably Mrs. McElvoy's age but looked much younger—was helping her toward the funeral home limo. A couple of news reporters were shouting questions at them, holding microphones as far over the caution tape as their arms would stretch. Mrs. McElvoy and her friend in the blue suit sailed past them without stopping, almost like jaded Hollywood celebrities.

The whole thing looked like a circus. Television cameras and newspaper reporters were everywhere, and

Halloran was grateful Pettus had stretched out the yellow tape as a boundary for the media. Since Carmelita Santos's disappearance had been made public, Cedar Hill had become a national news story. All three networks had converged on the town, and not to be outdone, CNN and Fox News had also set up shop. Several patrolmen were stationed around the scene, just in case anything got out of hand.

All three men surveyed the crowd of mourners, looking for anyone who seemed out of place or suspicious, but it was hard to tell. There were so many people, and most he felt sure were friends or family. There were quite a few children as well, most likely Sarah Jo's classmates, all huddled together in a somber group, some of them crying. Even the mayor had been here; he had given a small speech before the service (some drivel that had been captured for posterity by the news cameras) before being escorted to his car and whisked back downtown.

Chapman loosened his tie and blew out a breath. His freckled forehead was glistening in the heat. "See anything unusual?"

Halloran shook his head. "Other than the fact that we've got the TV news covering a Cedar Hill funeral, no." He looked over the crowd, wondering if, as he had suspected, Sarah Jo's killer might be mingling with the mourners, passing himself off as just another grieving friend.

"This is crazy," Pettus said. "I've spent my whole life in this area. I've never seen anything like it."

Chapman stared straight ahead, not looking at him.

"I'll be honest with you," he said. "This scares me."

Halloran glanced at him, then went back to studying the crowd. Chapman wasn't the only one who was scared. Halloran was more than a little uneasy himself. Hell, Cedar Hill hadn't had a murder in over ten years, back when he was still patrolling the streets. That was the Bollinger murder—the kid that had stabbed his grandmother to death before school one morning. Shane Bollinger. That was the kid's name. He'd been tried as an adult, but his attorney had skirted the death penalty by having him plead insanity. Now the kid (shit, he must be about thirty by now) was rotting away in some prison somewhere.

But that had been a family squabble. This was something else entirely, and if his instincts were correct, Carmelita Santos was already victim number two.

They had gone over all the possibilities with the Santos couple and the other people living in the house with them. Everyone's whereabouts could be accounted for during the time Carmelita had disappeared. And no one else in the neighborhood reported seeing anything or anyone usual. Chapman had raised the question of looking at the other migrant workers in the area, especially anyone who might have suddenly disappeared and grabbed the opportunity to take a pretty little Mexican girl with him. But so far, visits to local farm owners concluded that all their summer help was accounted for. There were absolutely no leads at all.

"What're you thinking about?" Chapman asked.

"Carmelita Santos."

Chapman nodded. "Me, too."

"Time's running out."

"Yep."

Halloran watched the news people scrambling about. He thought he recognized a couple of the reporters from TV, and he realized that none were from the local station over in Springfield.   "This is turning into something big," he told Chapman.   "One murdered girl is one thing, but now that another one is missing, I think the people of this town are going to demand some action. And they're going to want it real quick."

Halloran looked at his watch. A press conference was scheduled in front of the city hall for 3:00. Police Chief Pettus and Halloran would be detailing the efforts of the investigations so far, and Mayor Carver would be there for public reassurance. He hated these things, and luckily he had had to do very few over the years. But they were important, and sometimes they led to some very promising leads. He had to admit, though, that scheduling this conference was one of the few good things Pettus had done; he seemed to understand now the depth of what was going on, the magnitude of it. And that was surely good.

Halloran blew out a breath. "Guess we'd better get downtown and get set up," he said.

6:02 PM

All day Joel had been obsessing over his experience in the mayor's basement. And while he had to admit to being both alarmed and turned on by the red room with its suspended sling, he was mostly still wondering about the newspaper clippings and what they might mean. Could the mayor somehow be involved? Could he actually have killed Sarah Jo McElvoy? Why else would he have kept those articles?

Wade hadn't seemed to notice that Joel was preoccupied all afternoon, even though Joel failed to respond to Wade's inane conversation a couple of times. More than likely, Wade was too concerned with whatever he had been doing all weekend to worry over whether Joel was paying attention to him. Joel was fairly sure that Wade had probably been out with another woman; he didn't need to touch him to know that. And Marla knew as well; you didn't need to be psychic to know when your spouse was sleeping around.

Joel had microwaved a Hungry Man dinner, and he parked himself in the recliner with a TV tray and a beer, settling in to watch the news and eat his supper the way he did every night. He had just flipped on the television and scooped up a big forkful of mashed potatoes when the image blazed on the screen and he nearly knocked his tray over.

The mayor was on TV. He was standing behind a podium beneath a green tent, surrounded by flowers and men in dark suits. "I want to pledge to the people of Cedar Hill, and especially the McElvoy family, that justice will be served. The sanctity of our city's children has been violated, and we will take action." The tape cut back to a long shot, and Joel realized the mayor had been speaking at Sarah Jo McElvoy's graveside service. A chill went through him. The son of a bitch might have killed her, and here he was trying to bolster the public. The station cut back to the studio, and the female anchor began giving the story of another girl, Carmelita Santos, who had been missing since Saturday. There was another tape, this time a press conference on the steps of City Hall. The mayor was speaking again, and Joel could only stare at him, entranced by his wagging beard and his stone-dead eyes, wondering if he were looking at the face of a monster.

Then some detective came on, detailing what the police had managed to find out so far. It wasn't much, he admitted, and he was asking for any help the public could give, any tips or leads that might bear following up. The guy looked to be in his early forties, with thick dark hair and a mustache. His face was worn and haggard. Joel liked him at once; there was a sincerity to his voice, a grit in his demeanor that meant business. His name flashed on the screen: Michael Halloran. Joel scrambled to find a pen on the end table beside the recliner, and he scrawled Halloran's name down on his napkin.

When he looked up again, the tape of the conference was over and the TV was showing a picture of the Santos girl. She was a pretty, black-haired child, her dark eyes shining in happiness and innocence, and Joel immediately knew she was probably dead. There was no flash of visions, no alarming voices or smells. It was just a sudden knowledge, like knowing he'd left the mail on the kitchen table or knowing that he would look outside his window and see the cable truck sitting in the driveway. He just *knew*.

Before him, his dinner began to congeal, untouched.

* * *

All evening Joel was restless and anxious, turning over in his head what little he knew. Even when he finally was in bed, his mind refused to turn off. It was like some damned blaring radio that had no volume control and was stuck on the same station.

And then, just before midnight, it hit him. He would go see the mayor at his office. He would drop by City Hall on the pretext of following up on the new cable hookup, just to see if they were satisfied with the work he and Wade had done at the house.

And he would shake the mayor's hand.

11:55 PM

Sometimes on nights like this, he would go outside and stand naked in the yard, feeling the velvety touch of the summer night air on his bare skin. He would listen to the drone of insects, the occasional call of a whippoorwill, the soft hooting of an owl. He would feel the tickle of the grass beneath his feet, its surface wet with dew. He would sniff the heavy scents of earth and roses and, in the spring, cherry blossoms. Occasionally, when it was raining, he would stand in the downpour, letting the shower wash him clean and innocent as a newborn baby.

But tonight he had a mission, and he did not remain outside.

In a dark, dusty corner, buried beneath a mound of moldering junk was a rusting Maytag chest freezer. He had found it back in the winter, and on a whim, he'd plugged it in and was surprised to discover that it still worked. It was then that a plan had begun to fester in his mind.

He began with experiments on animals—stray dogs and cats mostly. He strangled them, then wrapped their bodies in old sheets before hiding them in the freezer. Even with the thermostat set a little above freezing, they remained remarkably preserved for several weeks. And when spring came and the river began to thaw, he took them there to dump them in the water. He took only one a day; he did not want to risk someone noticing a cluster of dead animals floating downstream all at once.

He knew then that it was time to go forward. He had thought about it for a couple of years. How he would do it. What it would feel like. He just didn't know who it would be. Not until that day in April when Sarah Jo caught his attention.

He'd seen her one afternoon as she passed the water treatment plant down by the river. He'd been there scouting out new places to fish, and he'd stopped to take a leak in the bushes. He heard her before he saw her; she was singing, some song by Miranda Lambert. He hid behind a tree as she passed by on the dirt road, swinging an instrument case in her fist as she walked. Her blonde hair was tied back in a ponytail, which bounced with her steps, and her jeans fit tightly around her buttocks, molded to them. He watched her until she disappeared. She never even knew he was there.

The next day he waited in the same spot, and she

came by again at just about the same time. Again he watched her, and again she didn't see him.

For a week he hid in the bushes and watched her every afternoon, planning everything he would do. And the night before he did it, he lay sleepless and sweating on top of his bed, his heart hammering with excitement, fondling the leather gloves he planned to use on her.

In the end, it had not gone as smoothly as he had hoped. For one thing, it had been raining; for another, Sarah Jo was a fighter. He had squeezed and squeezed her throat, but she refused to succumb. His rain-slick gloves couldn't get a good enough grip on her neck, and the more she struggled, the harder it became to hold her. He finally wrestled her to the ground and kept his knee on her back while he pulled out his pocket knife. She was screaming in terror, flailing her hands blindly at him. He held up her head by her hair and sliced her throat open. The screams stopped with a gurgle.

He truly had not wanted it to end like that. Cutting her made the whole ordeal almost pointless. He had ruined her. Now, however, it was too late.

At first he had worried about the blood. There was so much of it. But that night, after several hours of heavy rain, the river overflowed its banks there at the low spot by the treatment plant, and any traces of Sarah Jo's blood on the ground had been washed away with the muddy water. His clothes were another matter; in the end he drove to the lake and burned them in a bar-becue pit at a public picnic area.

Once he was home, he worked feverishly through the

*evening while the lightning flashed outside and the
thunder shook the walls. He had so much to do, and he
was terrified of being caught.*

*The first thing he did was to carefully remove Sarah
Jo's shoes, then her jeans and panties. The sight of her
nakedness sent a ripple of excitement through him, and
it took every ounce of his mental strength to keep himself from tearing into her. The second thing he did was
to take the sawed-off end of an old shovel handle
(which was roughly the same diameter as an erect pe-
nis) and insert it firmly in her vagina. It was a difficult
procedure; she was small and her flesh was dry.*

*With that done, he placed her into the freezer, posi-
tioning her carefully and covering her with a sheet,
then lowered the lid. He piled the junk back on top of
the freezer and left it for the night, taking her things
with him. He would burn them later. The instrument
case with the clarinet inside would be more of a problem; for the moment he hid it in the trunk of the car.*

*The next day when he was sure he would be alone
for awhile, he went back to her. Her skin was pale and
blotchy and a bit of blood and other fluids had leaked
from her torn throat and pooled into pink ice at the bottom of the freezer, but otherwise, she was perfect. He
wrenched the wooden handle from her, and saw with
breathless excitement that she stayed open, molded to
the shape of the wood, just as he had hoped. From a
small metal box on a high shelf, he pulled out a vinyl
dildo and worked it into her while he touched himself.
He did not take long; he was too excited.*

He used her several more times over the next few

weeks, but the thrill soon began to wear thin. For one thing, the fact that her throat had been cut detracted from her beauty; she was spoiled. At first he tried hiding her throat with an old scarf or a corner of the sheet, but it didn't help; he knew the cut was there, and soon it was all he thought about while he was with her. For another thing, he was terrified of being caught, of someone opening the forgotten freezer and finding her there.

So one night in the middle of June, he took her out for the last time. He looked her over for any loose hairs or threads that might be attached, then took his pocketknife and carefully scraped underneath her fingernails. If someone found her downriver, he wanted to be sure they would not be able to connect her with him.

He took her down to the same spot at the river where he had dumped the animals. For a terrifying moment, he was sure she wouldn't float, that she would sink to the bottom into the muck and someone would find her the next morning. But she did float. He covered her with loose branches and set her adrift, watching as the pile moved away from him in the moonlight, agonizingly slow.

He waited anxiously for the next few days, listening to the news for any word that her body had been found, but there was nothing. He began to breathe easier. Maybe she had drifted on down to the next county; maybe she would never be found.

But a week later during the Fourth of July fireworks those kids had stumbled upon her. Again he was terrified, sure that she would be linked to him, and he had braced himself for the arrival of the cops at his door. But there had been nothing so far. They were all perplexed. Although they had mounted a massive search of the shoreline on both sides of the river for more than a mile, they had been unable to find where he had dumped her. Their investigation seemed to have stalled.

Then, on Saturday, when he had been on his way to the park to have another look at the river landing, he saw Carmelita. She was walking along the deserted drive into the park, her long black hair trailing in the breeze, her hips moving seductively with her every step. He pulled up beside her. She noticed him and smiled. He asked her where she was going. To the park, she said. What a coincidence, he told her, so am I; I'll give you a ride. My name is Carmelita, she said when he asked, her tongue dancing across the syllables like a dream. That's beautiful, he said. She didn't seem to notice when he slipped on his gloves. Then, just inside the park gate, right beneath the sign that said $500 FINE FOR LITTERING, he turned and grabbed her throat. She was dead in just a couple of minutes.

Again he anxiously monitored the details of the investigation into her disappearance, but as before, he had been extremely careful. There had been no witnesses. No leads. No trace of her.

And now he opened the lid of the freezer and peered down into her angelic face. This was the second night he had visited her, and it almost seemed as if she became more beautiful each time.

"I'm here," he whispered. "There's no need to be

afraid. ”

TUESDAY, JULY 10

9:40 AM

For the first time in five years, Joel called in sick. He had not had much sleep last night; his mind had been too busy turning over what he would say to the mayor when he saw him today. So, when his alarm clock blared on at 6:00, he fumbled for the snooze and smacked it. And then again. And again. Finally, at seven, he called Wade. Half an hour later when Wade pulled into the driveway, Joel expected him to come to the door to check on him. He didn't, though; just climbed into the cable truck and drove away, barely giving the house a glance. Joel watched him from the front window and was relieved.

When Wade was gone, Joel took a shower, then sat at the kitchen table with his coffee and a cigarette. His heart was pounding dully but insistently. He had a few Lortabs from a visit to the dentist last year; he briefly considered taking half of one to calm himself. Then he thought better of it. This was one time when he wanted his senses sharp and unimpeded. He dressed in his cleanest uniform and ran a brush through his hair.

"Mayor Carver?" he said to the mirror. "I'm Joel Roberts from Cable-Com. Just wanted to make sure you were happy with our work yesterday." He extended his hand, trying to look natural as he did it. He had no idea what he would do or say after he took the mayor's hand. He only hoped he could stay in control of himself.

Outside, he looked at Wade's truck sitting beside his Explorer in the morning sun. He wondered if he should get in it, feel the wheel and the seats, see if he could pick up anything on his brother and what he had done all weekend. But he couldn't bring himself to do that. Part of it he suspected; the rest he didn't want to know.

In town he parked as close to City Hall as he could get. The city was still swarming with reporters, and they seemed to have all camped out on the City Hall lawn. He weaved his way through them, stepped through a metal detecting device, and entered the lobby of the building.

The mayor's office was directly in front of him. He cleared his throat and headed toward the door. His heart was hammering and his hands were shaking, and he cursed himself for not breaking off just a bit of a Lortab to take the edge off things.

Larry Carver's receptionist was a young blonde, and Joel wondered if she'd ever seen the sling in the mayor's basement. She looked up at him and smiled.

"May I help you?"

"I'm Joel Roberts. I'd like to see the mayor."

She nodded, the smile never leaving her face, though it seemed to have grown cold. "What did you need to see him about, Mr. Roberts?"

Her question momentarily threw him off guard. "I...we did some work for him yesterday at his house. I'm with Cable-Com. The cable company."

She nodded again. "Did he need to pay you for something? Do you have an invoice I can give him?"

"No," he said, working to keep his voice steady. "I just came by to make sure he was happy with everything."

She scribbled on a pad. "I can leave him the message that you came by."

"Look," he said, his composure beginning to slip a bit, "I'd just like to see him, okay?"

She put down her pen and gave him that cold smile again. "I'm sorry, but he's not here."

Joel felt his whole countenance fall. "He's not?"

"No. He's out of town at a meeting. Left this morning. I'm afraid he won't be back in the office until tomorrow."

Joel stared at her, and part of him wanted to say insanely, "I'll wait," just to wipe that distant smile from her face. But instead he said simply, "Tomorrow?"

She nodded. "Is there anything else I can do for you, Mr. Roberts?"

He shook his head, turning for the door. "I guess not," he said. "Just...give him the message."

Back in the lobby he took a seat on a bench and

watched the passersby for a little while, wondering what to do next. After a few moments, it came to him. He headed outside and down the street to the police station.

10:40 AM

Halloran had been buried in paperwork all morning, mostly stuff he'd neglected the past few days while he and Chapman were roaming around Cedar Hill. He had checked for any updates on the Santos girl, and when there was nothing new, he made a small note of it in his report and resumed work on his backlog. So when Camron stuck her head in his office door and told him he had a visitor, he welcomed the break.

He looked up from his desk to see a huge bear of a man in a Cable-Com uniform stepping through his door. The guy looked young, in his twenties, but his eyes seemed ancient and wounded. "Lieutenant Halloran?"

Halloran stood. "That's me," he said, offering his hand.

The big man looked at it, then down at Halloran's desk. "Sorry, I don't shake hands."

Halloran forced his expression to stay neutral. This was going to be interesting. He motioned to the empty chair across the desk. "Have a seat."

As the man sank into the chair—gracefully for such a large guy, Halloran thought—he cleared his throat. "My name is Joel Roberts," he said. "I work for Cable-Com here in town."

"What can I do for you, Mr. Roberts?" Halloran had pulled out a legal pad and a pencil, ready to take notes.

"I understand you're on the Sarah Jo McElvoy case."

Halloran froze. He looked at the man across the desk. "That's right."

Roberts' face was unreadable. "I think I may have found something interesting."

Halloran sat up straight. "Go on."

"Wade—that's my brother—the two of us work for the cable company. Yesterday we were running a new outlet in Mayor Carver's house."

Halloran listened as Roberts told his story—how while working a job at Mayor Carver's house he had stumbled upon a secret room with a sex sling, about finding a pile of newspaper clippings relating to the McElvoy girl's disappearance. Halloran took notes of it all, a sensation of both dread and excitement prickling at his neck. When Roberts finished speaking, Halloran laid his pencil down gently. "So you think the mayor may have something to do with this?"

Roberts looked at Halloran, then glanced away. "I don't know," he said. "I just thought I should tell you what I found."

Halloran looked at his scrawled notes. "Did your brother…"

"Wade."

"Did Wade see any of this?"

Roberts shook his head. "No. I never even told him about it."

"Why not?"

The big man looked at his hands. "I don't know. It

was just...too creepy." He opened his mouth to say
something else, then stopped.

"Yes?"

Roberts chuckled humorlessly. "Wade's got a big
mouth," he said.

"I see." Halloran looked down at his notes.

Roberts was watching him anxiously. "Do you think
it means anything? I mean, you *will* follow up on it,
right?"

Halloran set his pencil down on the pad. "Mr. Roberts, right now we can't afford to ignore any leads we
might get. All I ask of you is that you not tell anyone
what we talked about here today. Agreed?"

Roberts nodded. "Sure."

"You realize we have another missing teenager in
Cedar Hill."

"How could I not?" Roberts said. "It's all over the
TV and the radio."

Halloran studied his face, looking for any signs of
instability. But there were none. Just those dark,
haunted eyes. "Mr. Roberts, be assured that we will
check this out. And in the meantime, you hear of anything else that may help us, please don't hesitate to call
me." He slid one of his business cards across the desk
and Roberts took it. "Thanks for coming in." He
reached across the desk to shake the man's hand, then
remembered. "Any particular reason you don't like to
shake hands?"

A struggle of emotions flashed across the big man's
face. "Just a hygiene thing," he answered. "I have a
phobia about germs."

When Roberts had gone, Halloran sat looking at his notes, his mind playing through all his conversations with Carver. The mayor seemed like a rock-solid guy, genuinely concerned about both girls and how the situation was impacting the community. Still, sometimes the most stable individuals could snap and do the most atrocious things. Could it be possible that Larry Carver was involved in such a heinous thing?

He needed to talk to Chapman. And to the chief.

11:00 AM

Joel emerged into the sunlight, squinting in the brightness. He felt like such an idiot. Coming here and talking to Halloran was probably a bad idea. He was sure Halloran thought he was a wacko. Those notes he had taken were probably already wadded up in his trashcan.

He crossed the street and headed down the sidewalk toward the small lot where he had parked. The air was cooler today, not so heavy. A velvety breeze stirred the air with the scents of pine and fresh-mowed grass. Across town, the bells in the courthouse tower were chiming the hour. If he hadn't been so preoccupied he might actually be enjoying his time out. He snapped on his sunglasses and trudged on, trying to ignore the heaviness he felt in his chest.

"Joel!"

He spun around to see a young woman moving toward him, waving, her blonde hair dancing about her face. It took him a moment to recognize her, and then he suddenly remembered her from the group on Sunday. "Dana?"

Her smile grew broader as she reached him. "Hi! What're you doing?"

He shrugged. "Just taking care of some business."

"It's good to see you again," she said, and he could tell she meant it. "I didn't get a chance to talk to you much Sunday. What did you think of the group?"

He smiled. "It was all right."

"Kind of overwhelming at first, huh?"

"Yeah. Kind of."

"Will you come back?"

He looked at her, into her deep blue eyes. "Maybe."

She looked at her watch. "Hey, you wanna have lunch? I'm supposed to meet some friends at Gidalfo's, but I'm just really not in the mood. There's a little deli right over here. If you're hungry, that is."

He stared at her dumbfounded. A beautiful, vivacious young woman was asking him to lunch. He laughed. "Sure," he said.

* * *

The place was Parrothead's. The décor was early patio—plastic lawn chairs and tables with colorful umbrellas. Murals on the walls depicted beach scenes and stuffed exotic birds swung from the ceiling. Jimmy Buffett—who seemed to be the whole inspiration of the place—sang on the sound system. Their waitress brought drinks in brightly colored plasticware.

"Isn't this place a blast?" Dana said. "I discovered it during my freshman year. I love Jimmy Buffett."

"Me, too," Joel said. "I saw him in concert once."

"Really? How was it? I've heard his shows are pretty wild."

Joel laughed. "Well, the audience was anyway. Most everybody was drunk." He didn't tell her about being pressed up against everyone on the way out of the stadium, how the barrage of thoughts and images hitting him from all sides was so crushing that he was in tears by the time he reached the parking lot. How after that night he'd never again gone where there was a chance he might get caught up in a crowd. Not even to the movies.

Dana took a sip of her Diet Coke. "So what's your claim to fame?"

"I'm sorry?"

"You know, your talent. Your sensitivity. Me, I can read objects. Just like my mom and dad. Most everybody in the group can do that."

"Yeah, I can do that, too," Joel said. "Sometimes. Mostly I can read people—their thoughts and feelings, things in their past." Dana gave him an alarmed look and he laughed. "I can't just read their minds or anything," he said quickly. "I have to touch them first."

"I can't read everything," Dana said, stirring her ice with her straw. "It has to have some kind of emotional attachment to it. Jewelry, clothing, stuff like that. Money is the absolute worst; there's so much desperation linked to it."

"I've never picked up anything off money before," Joel said, amazed.

"You're lucky."

Joel unwrapped his straw and took a sip of his Coke.

"So what can some of the others in the group do?"

Dana thought for a moment. "Well, there's Deb, of course. She can pick up things from places—voices and feelings, not really visions so much."

"That's got to be a bitch," said Joel.

"What do you mean?"

"Well, the two of us, we can at least avoid touching things when we go someplace. It would be pretty awful to be bombarded by stuff all the time. It's only happened to me once or twice."

"I asked her about that once," Dana said. "She told me it was kind of like having a ringing in your ears. You just get used to it after a while, and you learn how to tune it out. Plus, I don't think she picks up stuff just from driving down the street or going into the grocery. There has to be some real feelings to the place."

Joel nodded. "I understand." He thought of Mayor Carver's basement, of the secret room and its sling. He shuddered. "Emotion seems to be the key to all of it, doesn't it?"

"She doesn't really talk about it much," Dana said, staring at the table. "I know that she had a breakdown as a teenager. Had to be hospitalized for a while. That was after a class trip to Gettysburg."

"Gettysburg? The battlefield?" God, Joel thought, that must have been horrible. He remembered his experience at the museum, and tried to imagine how a teenage girl would feel being assailed by the horror and sensations of thousands of Civil War soldiers. He couldn't even begin to understand how Deb must have felt, in spite of his similar experience. "She must have lost her mind," he said.

Dana nodded. "She just about did."

Their waitress brought their sandwiches, and Joel bit into his greedily. "What about the others?" Joel asked between bites.

"Well," Dana said, tearing open her bag of potato chips, "There's Joseph, the old guy. He and Barry can both see the future."

Joel stopped chewing. "Really? Both of them?"

Dana nodded. "I think Joseph's comes and goes. But Barry…"

"What about him? Father Michael said he's had some rough times. That he tried to kill himself."

"Yeah," Dana said softly.

"What happened?"

"Well, I only heard him talk about it once," Dana said. "It was one of the first times I'd been to the group, and it just about terrified me. I was almost too scared to go back."

Joel's curiosity was brimming. "What did he say?"

"He was living in Memphis with his fiancée. They'd been together about two years, and they were in the middle of planning their wedding. One night, out of the clear blue, he had a vision of her being murdered. Stabbed to death, actually."

"That's terrible."

"Yeah. He didn't know what to do. It was the first time he'd had a vision. He didn't know if he should tell her because he didn't want to upset her. And he wasn't sure it was even real. He just about lost it, worrying over it. In the end, he told her about it, and they just kind of laughed it off." Dana fell silent and took a sip of her drink.

"I don't have to guess how it ended," Joel said.

She nodded. "Barry was the one who found her. She'd been attacked in the parking lot of their apartment house. She managed to crawl to the back door, but she died before anyone could help her. They never caught the maniac who did it."

Joel was shaking his head in disbelief. "Poor guy."

"He began having more visions. Some pretty bizarre ones, I think. You remember Flight 800?"

"The plane that blew up over New York?"

"Yeah. He saw that a day before it happened. Nine-eleven, too. He tried to contact the authorities about it, but they ignored him, though he *was* investigated by the FBI after the fact. Now I'm sure they wish they'd listened."

Joel shivered. "Creepy."

"I think it was right after that he did it. Slashed his wrists. Luckily, he was late with his rent. His landlord showed up, found him bleeding to death in the bathtub."

Joel pushed his sandwich away. He suddenly wasn't very hungry anymore. "Well," he said. "I don't feel like such a freak."

Dana laughed. "I know what you mean."

"I take it he still has visions."

"I assume so."

"Has he ever had a vision about anyone in the group?"

Dana shrugged and popped a chip into her mouth.

"Not sure. If he had one about me, I don't think I would want to know."

"I hear you," Joel said. He watched Dana's hands as she picked up her sandwich, watched her lips as she bit into it. He wondered what he would discover if he touched her, what secrets in her heart would be revealed. He had begun to feel something stirring within him while sitting here with her. Something warm and exciting yet strangely terrifying. He was feeling a growing attraction to her, an attraction he hadn't felt for anyone in so many years. He wondered what she thought of him, if she considered him fat and gross. He tried not to think about that. He knew what he looked like, and he didn't need an inner voice—one that was starting to sound more and more like Clifton or Wade— reminding him. So, before he had a chance to stop himself, he blurted out, "Are you seeing anyone?" And when Dana looked up at him in surprise, he felt sure he had done the wrong thing.

"I'm sorry," he said. "I shouldn't have asked that."

"No," she said, smiling, "it's all right."

"I just say things before I think sometimes. I didn't mean to—"

"No."

He looked at her. "Excuse me?"

She smiled. "No. I'm not seeing anyone."

Joel felt his face grow hot. He tried to return her smile, but he couldn't meet her eyes. Instead, he found himself talking to his sandwich. "You seem like a really nice girl," he said. "I just get nervous when I talk to…" He trailed off, unsure of whether to say "girls" or "women." He cleared his throat. "I mean, if you wanted to, if you're not busy maybe we could—"

"Joel," Dana said, "are you asking me out on a date?"

His face and even his ears were white-hot. "Yes."

"Sure," she said. "I'd love to."

2:55 PM

Halloran and Chapman sat in the conference room looking over all the faxes that had been sent to them in the past few hours. After Joel Roberts had left the office, Halloran had ordered a criminal records check on him. He had also ordered one on Larry Carver.

But Halloran wasn't finding anything too unusual in either man's record. One speeding ticket in 1987 was the extent of Larry Carver's brush with the law. Similarly, Joel Roberts had had one DUI six years ago. That was it.

Halloran threw the papers on the conference table. "Nothing," he announced.

Chapman looked up from his files, shaking his head. "Same here."

Halloran fingered his cigarettes through his shirt pocket. Somehow, knowing he wasn't allowed to smoke in here made him need one all the more. "What do you make of the newspaper clippings?"

Chapman looked at him. "Weird." He chewed the tip of his pen. "What would he be doing with those?"

"Don't know." Halloran reached for his coffee. It was cold. "I'd give anything to see them for myself."

Chapman raised his eyebrows.   "You think this guy's telling the truth?"

Halloran shrugged and took a sip of the cold coffee. "I'd just like to see, is all."

"You think the mayor would consent to that?"

"Don't know."

"If he didn't, you'd need a search warrant."

"Yep."

"For the *mayor's* house."

"That's right."

Chapman leaned back in his chair.   "You've got some damned big balls, Mike."

11:15 PM

At ten-thirty he had come suddenly awake, thinking of Carmelita.   He thought of her black hair and her brown thighs waiting for him and instantly he was hard.

Carefully and quietly, so as not to wake anyone, he went to her.   And he knew it was the last time.   He had kept Sarah Jo too long, and he had left himself open to discovery.   He did not want that to happen again.   Even though Carmelita was smooth and beautiful as porcelain, he could not take chances.   So, as he touched her, he knew he was saying goodbye.   Knew this was the last time he would stroke her face and brush his lips across her breasts.   It was a beautiful moment, tender and poignant.

When he was finished, he quietly got dressed and began cleaning Carmelita up just as he had Sarah Jo.

He was very careful to brush her hair and to scrape beneath her fingernails with a knife. He combed out her pubic hair and her eyebrows, then wiped her skin down with alcohol. He folded the sheet up around her body. The river would take care of the rest of the evidence.

Sweat was pouring down his neck and chest, soaking through his shirt. He stopped to rest, looking at the shrouded body in the semi-darkness. He slid to the floor, never shifting his gaze.

He remembered the other day when he had seen her walking down the road toward the park, how instantly alive he had felt. The mere sight of her swaying hair, her light step, seemed to send a rush of desire, a hungering lust, through his veins. That urge, that need, more powerful than the instinct to breathe, had consumed him like fire. As soon as she smiled at him, he had known what he would do. What he would have to do.

Watching his hands inside the gloves was like watching the hands of a stranger. They seemed to be beyond his control, like small savage animals writhing in desperation. The feeling of her throat under his thumbs, however, even through the gloves, was enough to ground him in reality. The throb of her pulse—strong and quick at first like the heart of a bird, then slowing and erratic—pounded through him as if she were linked to him. Her fists flailed against him vainly, striking against his chest and giving his head a glancing blow. And as her gasping stopped and the light faded from her eyes, the sense of power, of lust, was stronger than ever in him, and he had to kiss her, even as the life ebbed from her.

And now, as he crouched in the darkness, looking at the shrouded form beside him, he realized he was weeping. Why had he done this? What was inside him that made him do it? And why was he so powerless to control it?

He wiped his eyes on the sleeve of his shirt. He had to get himself together. He had to stop crying and control himself.

He had work to do.

WEDNESDAY, JULY 11

8:05 AM

Wednesday morning, Edgar Castle and his wife, Wanda, had gone out on the river in their johnboat to get in some early fishing. It had cooled off considerably since the rain last week, and the fish were biting again. They had left a little before six, and Wanda had packed them a breakfast of sausage and biscuits, which they ate as they drifted downstream. The air was thick with swirling fog, and the golden sun was just peeking through the tree branches.

As they neared a slight bend close to Riverside Park, a cold breeze stirred over the water. It rushed past them up the valley, leaving them wondering if they'd really felt it at all. Later, Wanda Castle would remark to her friends that she felt "a goose walk over her grave."

Edgar had just cast out his line when he noticed something white floating in the water close to the landing. He squinted to see it through the fog. This was where Sarah Jo McElvoy's body had been found a week ago; the area was still roped off with yellow police tape. At first Edgar thought some kids had sneaked down to the river's edge to play a cruel prank by discarding an old mannequin at the crime scene. Then, as the boat drifted closer and the fog lifted a bit, he could see that the pale arm reaching up out of the brambles was fleshy and real.

Wanda saw it, too. She screamed before she could stop herself.

Beside her, Edgar was already dialing 911 on his cell phone.

9:30 AM

Within thirty minutes of the first officers responding to the scene, Halloran and Chapman pulled up to the edge of the bluff overlooking the river and parked between two cruisers with flashing lights. A female officer was sitting at a picnic table with an older couple that looked shaken and sick. They must have been the ones that called in.

As they made their way down the dusty slope toward the landing, Halloran saw the response team barricading the area with new tape. Johnson, the most experienced, had just finished photographing the scene. The girl's body bobbed close to the same spot where Sarah Jo had been found. Halloran shuddered uncontrollably.

Brooks, the first responding officer, met him on the landing. He was fresh-faced and eager and young; Halloran trusted him implicitly. There were very few of the younger guys that Halloran could stomach these days with all their strutting and loud mouths. Greg Brooks was different—soft-spoken yet confident. Halloran hoped one day to see him in the investigations unit. "What've you got for us?" Halloran said.

Brooks motioned up on the bluff. "The old couple found the body about an hour ago. They were fishing. Husband says he thought it was a prank at first, what with it being in the same place and all."

"Any ID on the body?"

"No, sir."

"Is it the Santos girl?"

Brooks nodded. "I believe so, Lieutenant."

Stepping across the landing, Halloran made his way toward the edge of the water. He could see the hand now, blue and hideous. Carefully, he reached over and pulled the dead branches off the face. Carmelita Santos' waxy eyes glared at the sky. Her throat bore the black bruises of strangulation. She was completely nude.

He pulled on a pair of surgical gloves and carefully moved her head to get a better look at her throat. The cold skin beneath his fingers slid greasily over the bone and cartilage below. He pressed softly on the fleshy part of Carmelita's thigh, and then he knew. This body had also been frozen, and it had not been here long; at least not long enough to thaw completely.

He stood and stripped off the gloves, carefully examining the shoreline around the body. He was just about to turn away when something caught his eye—a tiny glint in Carmelita's black hair. He knelt and eyed it closely. "Brooks."

"Yes, sir."

"I need an evidence bag."

"Be right back."

Halloran never moved. His gaze was still locked on the single blonde hair that was caught in Carmelita's tresses.

11:10 AM

Every time Joel thought about his date Friday night, his gut clenched in fear.

He had almost put it out of his head, had just about convinced himself he had dreamed the whole episode with Dana, when Wade said, "You oughta come out for a few beers with me Friday night."

They were driving down Chestnut Street, going toward the college, passing the bars and clubs that catered to the college kids, and Joel nearly ran the truck up on the sidewalk. It was the first time Wade had ever suggested the two of them do something alone. Joel glanced over, and Wade was staring intently at the old Capitol Theatre as they passed it.

Joel shifted in his seat, looking back at the street in front of him. "I can't."

"Why not? Gotta stay home to flog your log?"

Joel felt his face blush. "I've got a date."

He could feel Wade's eyes boring into him. "You gotta be shittin' me."

Joel smiled in spite of himself. "No. I swear."

"Anybody I know?"

"Nope." Joel pulled the truck over, parking in front of the next house on their work orders.

Wade was still staring at him. "So who is she?"

"Just somebody I met." He picked up the work order, pretending to check it over. He was not going to miss this opportunity to make Wade squirm.

"When in the hell have you been anywhere to meet somebody?" Wade pulled off his sunglasses and looked at him squarely. "Did you pick up one of those girls that hang around Fourth Street?"

Joel glared at him. "No."

Wade was smirking. "You answer one of those personal ads on the Internet?"

"No. It's nothin' like that." He climbed out of the truck and headed toward the house.

"Wait a minute." Wade caught up to him. "Just tell me where you met this girl."

Joel looked at him. "Church, all right? I met her at church."

Wade backed up. "Church? You don't go to church."

Joel grinned at him and rang the doorbell. Messing with Wade's head was fun.

* * *

By the time Joel got home, he was feeling pretty good about himself. Talking to Wade had made him realize how much he was looking forward to his date with Dana. Though he was still anxious about his first date in several years, it felt good just knowing he had something planned out to do, something to look forward to that didn't involve the TV or Wade.

Thinking of Dana, the memory of her laugh or her infectious smile, was enough to send a thrill shooting through him. When was the last time he had felt that way about anyone? Hell, when was the last time he'd even been interested in anyone? Certainly not since—

Did you know there were canals on Mars?

Not since that night.

Really?

Yeah. A long time ago they thought that meant there was water there. And life.

Real Martians?

Yeah.

Hey, Roberts!

He shuddered and forced himself to think of something—anything—other than that night.

He pulled a beer from the refrigerator and plopped down on the couch, grabbing the remote and punching on the TV. *Andy Griffith.* God, he loved this show. Barney Fife just killed him.

He wondered again about his visit to the detective yesterday. He hoped he hadn't come off as a nut, like some loser spouting off about government corruption and cover-ups, like Clifton. If Halloran had half the brains Andy Griffith did, that poor girl's murderer would have already been caught. But nobody ever died in Mayberry. Not even of natural causes. A murder there would be unthinkable.

Good old Andy.

Joel settled back into the couch, watching Andy and Barney locking up Otis again.

At some point, he fell asleep. He had to be asleep, because there he was, by God, standing right on the street in front of the sheriff's office in downtown Mayberry. Glancing down, he could see he was wearing a brown sheriff's uniform; the sunlight glistened off his badge. The streets and sidewalks were deserted, and not even a bird disturbed the silence.

He stepped into the office, and the door slammed behind him. His mouth gaped at what he saw. Barney had pulled Otis' head through the bars of the cell. He had him in a headlock, and his gun was pointed right at Otis' temple.

Except Barney wasn't Barney; he was Wade. And Otis was Clifton.

"Don't make me do it, Andy," Barney/Wade said.

Otis/Clifton looked at Joel with pleading eyes, eyes that filled with horror when Joel said, "Go ahead. Blast the fucker."

Barney/Wade pulled the trigger, and Otis/Clifton's head exploded.

Barney/Wade holstered his gun and straightened his shoulders, unaware of the blood and brains dripping down the front of his uniform. "Now," he said. "Now. Let's go look at Mars."

* * *

Joel jerked awake. His head was thick and fuzzy. He rubbed his eyes and reached for his beer. A laugh escaped him. He and Wade as Andy and Barney. He was going to have to remember to tell Wade about that one.

He glanced at the television and sat up rigidly. That

Mexican girl's picture was on the screen. He reached for the remote, but even before he got the sound turned up, he knew they had found her body.

Sure enough, the shaky video footage showed the shrouded figure being carried from the same spot where the McElvoy girl's body was discovered. Then Halloran was again giving a news conference, flanked between the police chief and another detective Joel hadn't seen. Right now there was no conclusive evidence that the two murders were connected, but he was urging the public to come forward with any information that might help the investigation.

He shook his head. What would he find now if he went back to the mayor's basement? Would there be a new set of newspaper clippings added to the first? And what would he find if he looked around a bit more?

For a few breathless moments, he seriously contemplated going back. He could always say he was checking something with the cable. Then, if he was sure he was alone, he could do some snooping. Check out the red room some more, look for anything out of the ordinary that might link the mayor to either girl. But he knew he couldn't do that. He'd already left a message for the mayor at his office yesterday; showing up on his doorstep might be a bit much. He didn't want Mayor Carver to think he was a stalker.

No, he told himself. He'd gone to the police. He'd told Lieutenant Halloran everything he knew. He'd done all he could. It was up to the cops now. Whatever happened was out of his hands.

6:25 PM

Halloran sat at his desk, the freshly-processed photos of the body dump site spread before him. They were eerily similar to the pictures in Sarah Jo McElvoy's file.

He stared at them, studying every object, as he had the others. There was no sign of any struggle at the water's edge, so Carmelita had obviously been killed somewhere else and dumped at the landing. Surely she had been brought there intentionally; the odds were just too great that her body had simply drifted downriver to rest in the exact spot as Sarah Jo's. But there were so many shoe prints and so much contamination of the scene from the last investigation that anything new would be hard to spot. He blew out an exhausted sigh and stacked the photos.

Mrs. Santos had not taken the news of her daughter's death very well. As soon as she spotted Halloran and Chapman at the door, she began wailing. It was a hideous sound, a cry of grief that seemed to emanate from her very womb. Other women in the house had led her away, eyeing the detectives as if they were demons. Halloran told Mr. Santos what they had found, and the man only nodded grimly, saying nothing, tears sliding silently down his cheeks. Finally, after a few moments of uncomfortable silence, Halloran and Chapman had left.

Halloran was devastated, knowing there was a murderer in town and that the department had been unable to stop him from killing again. He felt powerless, impotent. Would any more girls disappear? He hoped not. But how many more times would he uncover a young girl's body? How many more times would he have to stand before a mother and tell her that her daughter was dead?

He pulled out the photographs again, studying the dirt around the body. If Carmelita had been placed there deliberately, she had been carried; there were no tracks to indicate the body had been dragged. That would mean whoever they were looking for was an extremely strong individual; Carmelita was not fat, but she was fairly stocky, and an average-sized man would have a difficult time carrying her down the rocky bluff to the landing.

He looked at the river behind the body. Could she have been dropped there from a boat? The water was relatively shallow at the landing, and many years ago a sightseeing boat used to moor there. It would not be easy to dump a body from a small boat without danger of capsizing, but it could be done. The nearest boat ramp was about ten miles upstream at Caneyville, so a person would have to haul a boat there and cast off from a public fishing area, an act certain to attract attention in the middle of the night. If a boat had been used, it was likely something small that could be launched off the riverbank. And if that were so, a search of the banks upstream should reveal some evidence.

He had just reached for the phone to call Chapman when it rang, startling him. Scotty's voice on the other end was cracking with excitement. "We've got a match on the hair you found," he said.

Halloran sat up straight. "Sarah Jo's?"

"Yep. Just got the call from the lab."

"Great work."

"Hey, you're the one who found it."

Halloran hung up the phone and stared at it while he fondled his cigarette pack. It was time to organize another search of the riverbanks.

8:15 PM

Wade was sprawled in the recliner, sipping a beer and leafing through a J.C. Whitney catalog. Poring through page after page of Mustang parts and accessories made his mouth water with anticipation. Thinking about what he and Derek could do to the car was almost more fun than actually working on it. But damn! By the time he got everything they needed for it, he would almost spend another four grand.

Across the room, Marla sat cross-legged on the sofa. The TV was blaring some sitcom, and the television audience was roaring with laughter. Marla stared empty-eyed at the screen; she was not paying any attention to the show and he could tell. He looked at her above the edge of the catalog, watching her pretend to look at the TV and biting on her nails. What the hell was she thinking about? Where was her mind?

It was times like this that he almost feared her, when she just blanked out like she was now, though he would never let her know that. Knowing how much she hated him sometimes, how little they got along anymore, he wondered if she was considering leaving him. Or something worse.

He had been so pissed when he found out she had

called Joel. He wanted to go off on her, but by the time he got home from work he was too tired to get into it with her. He hadn't mentioned it, and neither had she. But God help her if she ever did it again.

His phone rang, jarring him from his thoughts. Marla looked over at him, then turned back to the television. He glared at her as he picked it up. "Yeah."

"Hello, handsome."

It took him a moment to place the voice, and then he realized it was Abby. "Hey."

"What's up?"

"Not much," he said. "Just watchin' TV."

"You comin' out Friday night?"

"I might."

"We'll be there around nine. I get off work at six, but Shelley's got to stay 'til seven-thirty."

"Well, that sucks."

She laughed. "Tell me about it." There was a pause, and she said, "Hey, guess what this sound is." He strained to hear a slight raspy, bristly sound. "You hear that?" she said.

"Yeah, what was it?"

She giggled. "I was touching myself. Thinking about you."

His face grew hot and he felt a sudden twinge between his legs. "Yeah?"

"Mmm-hmm. Still doing it, too." She let out a slight sigh.

Wade shifted uncomfortably in his chair, trying to accommodate his growing erection. "Really?" He eyed Marla, who was still staring at the television.

"Yeah. But I sure wish it was your fingers instead of mine."

It was all he could do to swallow. "Me, too."

"Are you touching yourself, too?"

"You bet," he lied, wishing to God Marla would leave the room. If she would just go to the bathroom, or go wash the fucking dishes.

"I wish I was there. Watching you do it. Watching your big strong hands giving yourself pleasure. Maybe I could use my mouth. Would you like that?"

"Uh-huh." He froze. Marla was staring at him, her eyes boring through him. He shifted the catalog so she couldn't see the bulge in his pants. "It's Joel," he mouthed to her, and she nodded and looked back at the television. "Go on," he said into the receiver.

"I can't wait 'til Friday night," Abby was saying. "Can you come over now? We wouldn't have to tell Shelley. She won't be home 'til almost midnight."

"I can't," he said.

"Please? I'm going crazy over here. I want you so bad."

"Same here," he said. "But tonight's not good."

She sighed. "All right," she said sullenly. "But Friday you could come by early, before Shelley gets home. We could have some fun, just the two of us."

"You bet," he said. "We'll push the envelope."

Marla looked at him as he ended the call and Wade shook his head. "If he don't leave me alone about working on this goddamn car…" He opened the catalog back up and took a drink from his beer. His hands were shaking. He pretended to study windshield washer fluid reservoirs.

Finally, after an eternity, Marla looked away, back toward the television.

9:45 PM

Carmelita's body coming to rest at the same spot on the riverbank had been brilliant, even though it had just been a stroke of luck.

Last night when he got himself together he had carried Carmelita out to the car and had driven to his spot. The water was deep here and alive with the croaking of frogs. First he scoured both sides of the river, making sure he was alone. Then he dragged her out of the car toward the bank. She was still stiff, and it was an effort to maneuver her. He poised her on the edge, and the sheet around her unfurled as she tumbled freely to the water below with a hollow splash. With shaking hands, he lit a cigarette and watched to make sure she floated, not taking a drag until he could tell she was drifting downstream. Then he balled up the sheet and threw it into the car. Sweat was pouring off him in the heavy air. Quickly checking the weed-choked path behind him, he started the car and coasted out to the highway, where he switched on his lights and headed east toward the lake.

About five miles before the entrance to the state park, he turned off the main road and headed back into the darkness, where the thick undergrowth of the woods hugged tightly to the gravel lane he followed. Ten minutes later, he pulled into the driveway of an aban-

*doned farmhouse and grabbed the sheet from the back
seat. On the backside of the house was an old well, its
wooden cover gray and splintered with rot. He lifted
the edge of the cover and threw the sheet into the
blackness beneath. He didn't hear a splash, and he
wondered if the well had gone dry, if perhaps that was
why the house had been left empty.*

*As he stepped back into the car, a sparkle on the
floorboard caught his attention. It was a crucifix. For
a moment he was puzzled. Then he remembered it dangling from Carmelita's neck as she slid into the
passenger seat, and how he had caught his thumb in the
chain as he grabbed her. He held the crucifix before
him; Jesus' agonized eyes were black and hollow. He
shuddered, then looked away and shoved it into his
pocket.*

*Now, back in the solace of his special place, he held
it up before him. He touched it lightly with his fingertip
and watched it spin. Jesus' eyes caught his.*

Jesus was watching.

THURSDAY, JULY 12

8:30 AM

Pettus rubbed his temples and leaned back in his chair. Halloran's reports were spread out on the desk before him, and both sets of photos of the body dumpsite were in his lap. He looked from one pile to the other. His black eyes seemed to have sunk deeper into his brown face the last couple of weeks.

Halloran sat upright. His tongue tasted his lips for any leftover nicotine. He blew out a breath and took the last swallow of cold coffee from his cup. Beside him, Chapman chewed on his thumbnail and bounced his leg.

Pettus plopped the photos down on top of the reports. "I'll say this, Mike. You've got some damned big balls."

Chapman snorted, then covered it with a cough.

Halloran looked at him, then back at Pettus. "Yeah, so I've been told."

"There's no way a judge will give us a warrant for the mayor's house based on what you've got. There's no evidence linking him to the girls. None at all."

"I know that," Halloran said. "I just want your permission to talk to him."

"I don't know, Mike." He ran a large hand over his closely-cropped hair. "This department's been on rocky ground with Carver since his wife got a ticket for parking in a handicapped zone. I'd hate to do anything to piss him off again. He does control our budget, you know."

Halloran nodded. He liked Pettus, he really did. He was fair, and he was smart. As the first African-American police chief in Cedar Hill, he had dealt with considerable controversy during his tenure. Cedar Hill was by no means a racist community, but many in the town—mostly old-timers—had given Pettus a rough way to go; they apparently didn't believe Cedar Hill was ready for a black police chief. He had endured everything from indifference to outright hatred. Things had peaked during a city council meeting in which two councilmen (one black, one white) erupted into a fistfight over Pettus' firing of a white officer. Only after the mayor stepped in and publicly gave his unconditional support for Pettus did things in the city calm down. Halloran could certainly understand why Pettus wished to remain on Carver's good list.

"How about this," Chapman said. "We just talk to him about the investigation, how things are going. Kind of feel him out."

"That's fine," Pettus said, "so long as you don't insinuate anything. You all just remember—we have no evidence linking him to these girls. Nothing." He looked hard at Halloran. "Be careful."

Halloran swallowed. "I will."

Pettus stacked up the reports on the desk. "In the meantime, you said you want another search of those riverbanks. I agree. Let's go ahead and do it. And I'm going to call in the state for assistance. We need to find something. Anything."

10:30 AM

Marla had been in a stew ever since Wade and Derek left for work. Earlier it was easy to keep her mind off of things as the two of them rushed around in their frenzied morning routines. But after Joel picked up Wade and Derek spun out of the driveway toward town, after she sat down in the living room with a second cup of coffee to relax a bit before starting the laundry, after she turned off the *Today* show because she couldn't take any more of Savannah Guthrie's damned perkiness, she had started to brood.

Wade was seeing someone. She knew it. It wasn't just a one-time fling like he usually had. This was different. She didn't know how she knew, but she did. Was it that girl whose number she had found in Wade's pocket? Missy? Or was it someone else? And why did she even give a damn? One thing was sure: whoever she was, she had been with Wade last weekend. Wade wasn't even trying to hide it. He wasn't even pretending he was out doing something else.

She took a sip of coffee and her gaze fell on the side table. Wade had left his phone. She remembered Joel calling last night, and she wondered if he had ever told Wade about her frantic call Sunday morning. If so, Wade was keeping it a secret—she couldn't even begin to guess why. Maybe Joel hadn't said anything to him. But then Joel had seemed angry. Joel had—

Marla set down her cup and picked up the phone. Before she could stop herself, she looked at the call log. Maybe Joel *hadn't* called last night. Maybe it was Missy. Or someone else. Her heart pounded, and her hands had begun to shake. *555-4376.* She jotted it down.

That wasn't Joel. Was it Missy? She couldn't remember. She hit redial, and as the phone on the other end began to ring, a sharp pain began to throb in her temple.

The call connected. Voice mail. Two girls. Giggling.

"Hi, this is Abby—"

"And Shelley!"

"Please leave a message." There was more giggling followed by the beep.

Marla disconnected the call. She stared at the phone until tears blurred her vision, then hurled it across the room. It slammed into the wall, leaving a mark.

So which one was he fucking, Abby or Shelley? Or both? She paced blindly around the room, sobbing, banging her fists against the sides of her head. Damn him! God*damn* him! To think he had been talking to the bitch, right in front of her. What a fool she was, what an idiot. And why was she surprised? Wasn't it just like him?

Ignoring the tears sliding down her cheeks, she trudged upstairs to the bathroom and grabbed the laundry hamper. She pulled the damp towels from the rack and added them to the pile of dirty clothes, then lugged the basket out across the hall to Derek's room.

She blew out a disgusted breath. Papers, clothes, CDs, magazines. . . everywhere she looked was a pile of crap. Here was a plate with petrified pizza crusts on it. An empty Butterfinger wrapper peeked out from beneath the dresser. The mini-blinds in the window hung cock-eyed, like a drunk had tried to raise them. She shook her head. Why did she even bother? Why did she even bother living?

She sank to the bed. Fresh tears stung her eyes. One of Derek's shirts lay rumpled among the sheets. She pulled it to her face and dabbed at her cheeks. The shirt smelled of Derek— Irish Spring soap and Tag body spray and the faint hint of masculine sweat. Her little boy had become a man. She buried her face in the shirt.

She could just take off for somewhere today. It didn't really matter where. No one would even know she was gone until late this evening, and by then she would be miles away. Wade probably wouldn't even come looking for her. And her parents most likely wouldn't give a damn. But Derek. . . she just couldn't leave Derek. And Derek wouldn't leave Wade. He still loved and admired his dad; he hadn't yet learned what an asshole Wade was.

She wadded up the shirt and tossed it into the laundry basket. Her gaze fell on Derek's computer in the corner. The screensaver was flashing pictures of bikini-clad models posing and cavorting on a beach. She watched it for a moment, remembering something Derek had shown her once on the internet. The phone number she had jotted down was in her jeans pocket. She pulled it out and stepped over a pile of magazines toward the desk and flopped into the chair. She chewed her lips as the modem connected with a series of squelches and beeps. She hoped she remembered the website Derek had pointed her to. She typed in the address and the page blazed onto the screen. Her shaking fingers keyed the telephone number into the search block, and in thirty seconds she had Abby's last name. A few more keystrokes and she had a street address.

Now she knew where the bitch lived. She stared at the monitor. A smile had crept onto her lips.

1:30 PM

God, it was hot.

Halloran had loosened his tie and unfastened the top button of his shirt. Sweat was trickling down his neck and pooling in the hollow of his throat. He wiped his forehead on the sleeve of his shirt and parted a clump of tall weeds with the toe of his shoe. Nothing there. He took a gulp from the lukewarm bottle of water in his hand.

All around him other members of the search team— some of them state boys—were carefully combing the riverbanks. They had started at the landing by the park and were working their way upstream on both sides of the river to Caneyville State Park. So far they had come almost a quarter of the ten-mile distance. Several bags of items had been collected—mostly trash—but anything that might link to a suspect, whether it be a candy wrapper or a foam cup, could turn up here.

Across the sluggish water, Chapman's red head bobbed among the tangled vines and limbs. Chapman's intensity for the investigation was impressive. Since Sarah Jo's body had been pulled from the river he had spent every hour at the office going through the evidence, had spent many late evenings looking at photos and following up leads. Halloran couldn't help feeling proud; he'd trained Chapman after all. He was becoming a good detective, and his drive and conscientiousness were innate traits that couldn't be learned in a police academy. He would be a natural to head up the whole department someday.

"Lieutenant!" One of the state guys stood in a small clearing. He beckoned Halloran closer and pointed to the ground. "Got something here."

Halloran climbed up the bank toward the officer. The bank was steep here, and he almost lost his footing in the loose soil.

Atop the knoll was a set of tire tracks. They weren't fresh, but they couldn't be more than a couple of days old. The ground had been soft and muddy when they were made, and now the treads were preserved perfectly in the hard dirt.

"Excellent," Halloran said. "Take an impression and get it to the lab."

He blew out a breath and took another sip of water. Onward and upward.

5:05 PM

Derek had just spent eight hours of hell in the kitchen of the Dairy Queen on Fourth Street. He punched his timecard and emerged into the blinding sunlight. It was hotter out here on the asphalt parking lot, but not by much. He hated it here—fucking hated it. The days were all a massive blur of flipping burgers, mopping floors, and scraping the grill. Half the time he couldn't remember what he'd done all day, as if he was just a functioning robot.

Today he happened to glance at the front line and spotted his old algebra teacher, Hicks the Prick, at the register. The Prick ordered a grilled chicken sandwich, which had to be cooked special. Derek spit on the meat before he tossed it over the flames. He would have been fired had anyone seen him, but nobody did. Frankly, he didn't care. If he got fired it might be the best thing to happen to him. But he had to admit, watching The Prick walk away with his tainted sandwich gave him a real feeling of satisfaction.

He jumped into the oven of his car and started it. Godsmack came blaring out of the speakers. Derek put the air conditioner on maximum and sat there with his eyes closed. The hot air blew in his face, and the bass of the music pounded through him, almost like a massage.

When the air finally cooled, Derek popped on his

sunglasses and headed down the street toward home. Tonight he was looking forward to watching some TV and just vegging. He was off tomorrow, thank God, and he hoped to catch up on his sleep.

He glanced at the dash and noticed his gas gauge was on empty. Fuck. So much for his last twenty dollars. He wheeled into the Gas-N-Pack on the corner and pumped in what he could. If gas got much higher he'd have to get a horse. He pulled his wallet from his back pocket and headed toward the store.

That's when he saw her. He didn't know who she was, but four words floated through his mind: "*fine piece of ass.*" Her angelic face was framed by dark curls that bounced with her step, and as she stepped through the door in front of him, his gaze fell on the mound in the back of her jeans. At the same time, he caught her scent, feminine and clean, and he wondered if he smelled like a sweaty deep fryer.

He moved down one of the aisles of the store and pretended to look at chips and candy bars. She was at the drink fountain filling a cup with ice and Mountain Dew. Another girl—a *sista*, not nearly as perfect as the angel he was following—came up behind her. "Hi, girl!"

The angel turned and gave her a smile that melted Derek to his core. "Hey!" she said. "I haven't seen you since last semester. How'd you make out with econ?"

The sista shook her head and waved her hand. "Tell you what, if you hadn't helped me I'd've flunked that class for sure." She pulled out a cup and began filling it. "So what're you doing this summer?"

"Taking some classes," the angel said. "I already took two and now I'm taking two more, and then I can graduate in December and not have to wait 'til the spring."

The sista shook her head. "You better than I am. Summer classes suck. You still living on campus?"

The angel snapped a lid onto her cup and stabbed it with a straw. "Nope. Shelley and I got an apartment over on Woodside. Nice old place. Big rooms and cheap rent."

The angel and the sista headed toward the register to pay. They were still chatting, not paying him the least attention. He moved up behind them and watched as they paid and walked out. He flung two tens at the Indian behind the counter and followed the girls into the heat of the lot. He heard them saying goodbye as he reached his car, and when the angel pulled out into the traffic in her Volkswagen Beetle, he was right behind her.

He followed her through several traffic lights and a couple of turns, and when they made a right onto Woodside, he felt his heart start hammering in his chest. He eased off the accelerator and put some distance between them, then slowed to a crawl when the Beetle pulled to the side of the street in front of an old Victorian house. That had to be her apartment building.

He sped up and drove past her just as she was getting out of her car with her drink and a stack of books. She never even looked up at him.

He sat at the stop sign on the corner and watched her in the rearview mirror as she headed toward the building and disappeared. His heart was still pounding, and he wondered how he would ever manage to see her again.

5:45 PM

Mayor Larry Carver sat down behind his massive desk and motioned for Halloran and Chapman to take the two overstuffed leather chairs opposite him. "So what can I do for you gentlemen? How's the investigation going?"

"We're getting a few leads," Halloran said.

Carver nodded. "Excellent, excellent."

Halloran took a deep breath. He knew he was going to have to be careful. "I need to ask you something, Mayor."

Carver shrugged. "Certainly."

"It's a bit. . . personal."

Carver stiffened, though his expression remained neutral. "Yes?"

"We've received an anonymous tip that you have a collection of newspaper clippings in your basement. Clippings about the McElvoy case."

Carver blinked. "What do you mean, 'anonymous tip?'"

Chapman shifted uncomfortably in his seat. Halloran glanced at him, then met the mayor's steady gaze. "We're following up any and all possible leads, no matter how far-fetched they might seem."

Carver's eyes narrowed. He looked back and forth between Halloran and Chapman. "Am I being accused of something?"

"No, sir," Halloran said, holding up his hand.

"Because if I am, you better make damn sure you know who you're dealing with here."

"No one's accusing you of anything," Halloran said. "We're simply asking a question."

Carver leaned forward and drummed his fingers on the desk. "Yes. I've got the clippings. I keep newspaper clippings on anything that could potentially impact the city's image. It's part of my job."

Halloran nodded. "I understand."

Carver gave him a hard look. "I don't think you do. You think this is a cushy job? That all I do is go around making speeches and cutting ribbons?"

"No, sir, I—"

"You have no idea what it takes to run a town the size of Cedar Hill."

"I'm sure I don't."

"I have to know *everything* that goes on in this city. I have to be able to market this town."

"I get it," Halloran said. Carver's face was blossoming red, and Halloran knew he had hit a nerve. "Like I said, we're just following up on a tip. Surely you must understand that we've got to cover all the bases."

"Sounds like someone's got too much time on their hands." Carver stood. "I think it's time for you leave."

Halloran blew out a breath. "So I take it you wouldn't consent to a search of your home."

"Get out of here before I call your chief and have you both thrown off the force."

Chapman was already on his feet and out the door.

Halloran stood and nodded at Carver. "Have a good evening."

Chapman was waiting for him in the hall. A smirk played across his lips. "That could have gone better."

9:08 P.M.

Joel twisted the cap off his second beer and sank into the recliner. He picked up his phone and stared at it, then set it back on the arm of the chair and took a sip from the bottle. He had told himself he would call Dana, just to make sure everything was still on for tomorrow night, but every time he started to punch in her number, panic seized his gut. He had been struggling with himself for half an hour now and had already drained one beer trying to settle down. But hell, it wasn't like he went out on dates all the time. This was new territory. New experiences for Joel.

On the television, an old Chuck Norris movie was playing with the sound off. Chuck Norris never had women problems he would bet.

With his heart thudding dully, he took one more drink of beer and keyed in Dana's number before he could stop himself. And when she answered on the third ring, time seemed to stop. "Hello, Dana?"

"Hi, Joel." She sounded pleased to hear his voice. "What's up?"

"Not much. Watching TV. Just got out of the shower."

"You're not calling to break our date are you?"

"No!" he said, a little sharper than he meant. "I

wanted to make sure we were still on for tomorrow night."

"Of course. Wouldn't miss it."

He smiled. "I'm looking forward to it, too."

Later, as he lay in bed, staring into the blackness, he remembered her soft hair and the way her nose crinkled when she smiled, and he found himself thinking he could really fall for this girl. He pictured the two of them going on more dates, actually being a couple. The thought both thrilled and terrified him. A week ago he hadn't even considered such an idea. Love seemed as likely to find him as a winning lottery ticket. He realized he was smiling.

The passing lights of a car played across the darkness of his bedroom, and as he caught a glimpse of the crack in the ceiling, he again thought of Mars.

Did you know there were canals on Mars?

He clutched his head in his hands. He would not think about this. He would not.

Real Martians?

His stomach burned with fire. He took a deep breath and forced that night from his mind. Nothing was going to spoil his thoughts of Dana. Especially not that. He closed his eyes and pictured her and soon he was drifting into sleep.

FRIDAY, JULY 13

8:35 AM

Derek wiped a sweaty strand of hair off his forehead and took a sip of his watery Dr Pepper. Fuck, it was hot. He leaned back in the seat and hung his head out the window, straining to catch even the slightest hint of a breeze.

At seven-thirty he had awakened and thought immediately about the angel he had seen yesterday at the Gas-N-Pack, and once she was in his head he knew it would be impossible to get back to sleep. He lay there listening to his mom and dad down in the kitchen, talking and arguing until the cable truck roared up in the driveway and honked and Wade burst out the back door. When he heard the TV blare on, he crawled out of bed and pulled on some clothes. As he passed through the kitchen on his way out the door he called, "I'm going into town," and emerged into the heavy air.

He climbed into his Escort and headed toward Cedar Hill, stopping at the 7 Eleven on the edge of town for a drink and a package of donuts. He drove through the bustling morning traffic toward the college campus and turned onto Woodside, and when he saw the house and the angel's car parked in the drive, he pulled over to the side of the street about half a block away. He positioned himself where he could keep an eye on the house and car in his side mirror, and he had been here ever since. In the last forty-five minutes, only two vehicles had passed by.

He had no idea why he was sitting here like some damned stalker. It wasn't like he was actually going to go up and talk to her. Somehow, just sitting here close to her house where he might catch a quick glimpse of her was almost enough. But if nothing happened in the next thirty minutes, he was heading back home.

He had just pressed the cold cup against the side of his face when movement caught his eye. It was her. The angel. She had walked around the corner of the building and was just getting into her car. He watched as she perched a pair of sunglasses on her face and backed out into the street. She passed by without noticing. He started the engine and pulled out behind her, staying as close behind as he dared. He certainly didn't want her to see him following her.

They passed through several lights and she pulled into a parking lot on the campus. The lot was by permit only, but after coming this far he wasn't going to just drive on. He whipped in behind her and took an empty space a couple of rows away.

He hunkered down in his seat as she got out of her car, locked it, then shouldered her book bag and headed for the cluster of buildings that comprised the campus quad. He wasn't sure what to do now. Should he follow her? He sure as hell didn't want to sit and roast in his car, and otherwise this whole thing had been pointless.

He eased out of the Escort and watched her cross the street. He followed. She tossed her long curls and greeted several other students as she made her way along the walk. He wondered what the other people on campus would think of him roaming around, but no one seemed to pay him any attention. Everyone was either intent on making their way to class or clustered in small groups talking. He took a deep breath and walked on.

The angel slipped into the Social Sciences building and disappeared. For a brief moment he thought of going in, but he stopped himself. She was going to class. He couldn't very well go in there without attracting some attention. There was a bench over by the walk in the shade. He took a seat and sipped his drink. He would just stay here for a little while. It wasn't too hot and there was a good breeze. He leaned back on the bench and waited.

10:15 AM

Halloran had drained his coffee cup. He sat staring at the computer monitor in front of him, looking over the crime scene photos of the Santos girl's dumpsite. He'd been studying them for a good half hour, enlarging them and searching for any small thing they could have missed. So far he was coming up with zilch.

He rubbed his eyes. They felt weak and strained. He pushed away from the desk, grabbed his cup, and headed down the hall for more coffee. As he rounded the corner, Chapman nearly ran him down. "Slow down, cowboy."

Chapman's eyes were bright and excited. "I was just coming to see you. We got something." He was waving around a sheaf of papers. "The tire track we lifted by the river? The tread belongs to a Michelin Cross Terrain tire. Standard on the Lincoln Navigator."

Halloran studied Chapman's face. "Something tells me you've got more."

"Guess who has a Lincoln Navigator? Larry Carver."

Halloran felt his stomach drop to his knees. "You're kidding."

Chapman headed back down the hall. "I'm going to see the chief. I think we got enough for our warrant."

11:08 AM

He had been planning what to say to her for the past hour. The Dr Pepper had finally run through him, and he'd made a mad dash to the nearest building to take a leak, terrified he would miss her while he was gone. He had taken as little time as possible in the restroom and had dribbled urine down the front of his shorts in his haste, but he tried not to care. He wanted to catch her when she headed back to her car. "Great day," he was going to say, and when she responded he would ask her name. What happened after that, he had no idea. He would just go with it.

He sat up straight. The angel had emerged from the building and popped on her sunglasses, squinting in the bright sunlight. She was heading toward his bench. This was it. His heart thudded dully in his chest. He stood.

She was just a few feet from him, and Derek had opened his mouth to say "Great day," when her cell phone rang. She stopped to dig it out of her bag and answered it, brushing past him without a glance. He watched her walk away from him, his lips still parted to say the words.

He expected her to head toward the parking lot, but instead she crossed the grassy quad toward the library. On impulse he followed. She was still chatting on the phone and laughing girlishly as she climbed the steps and pushed through the double doors.

He stood on the walk for a moment, then followed her into the library. The cool air and scent of old books greeted him. The workers behind the front desk were busy with paperwork. No one saw him. He spotted the angel as she disappeared behind the far shelves, and he headed toward her.

"Hey," said a male voice off to his right. He turned to see a slender bearded guy with glasses and a black knit cap looking at him.

Derek froze. "What?"

"Like your shirt," the guy said, nodding toward him.

Derek looked down and realized he was wearing a

Green Day t-shirt. "Thanks," he said.

"My favorite band."

Derek glanced back toward the corridor behind the shelves. "Really?"

The guy leaned forward. "Are you in my psych class?"

"No," Derek said. "Sorry." He moved on toward the shelves, craning his neck to spot the angel.

Just when he was afraid he had lost her, he heard her laugh, and turned just in time to see her slide into one of the study cubicles in the corner. She hung up her phone and starting pulling books out of her bag. He watched her from behind one of the shelves for a moment, and when she had settled in he approached her. "Hey," he said.

She looked up, and his breath was nearly taken away by her green eyes. She gave him a puzzled smile. "Hey, yourself," she said, and her voice was like music.

"Great day," he said. "Outside, I mean."

Her smile grew wider, and she tried to hide it. "Do I know you?"

"I don't think so." He moved up beside the cubicle. "I'm Derek. Derek Roberts."

"Hey, Derek Roberts," she said. "I'm Abby."

Abby. An angel named Abby. "So," he said, "how's it going?"

"Just got out of calculus." She motioned to the pile of books and paper spread out in front of her. "Got some problems to work on before I grab a bite to eat and head to my next class."

"Want some company? For that bite to eat, I mean."

She smiled at him again. "Look, you're cute, but I'm seeing someone right now." She looked back at the desk. "And I've got a ton of stuff to do."

He nodded. "Sure." He grabbed one of her note-books. A pen was stuck into the spiral and he uncapped it. "I'll give you my phone number."

She blew out an amused breath. "That's okay, I don't— "

"You might change your mind," he said. He jotted down his cell number on the front cover, then handed it back to her.

She took it with a smirk. "What did you say your name was again?"

"Derek Roberts."

She smiled and turned away. "I've really got to get to work, Derek," she said. She turned away from him.

"I hope I hear from you," Derek said, stepping back, and when she didn't respond, he turned and headed out of the library. He wasn't exactly sure what just happened, but he felt like an idiot.

3:34 PM

Halloran stood with Chapman and two police officers outside Larry Carver's office, drumming the rolled-up warrants against his closed fist. He could see Carver through the office window; he was talking on the phone, standing behind his desk and shooting them black looks over the top of his reading glasses. Halloran met the mayor's eyes. *He knows*, Halloran thought. Carver's secretary busied herself with her files, but Halloran could tell she was only pretending to work. She had barely spoken to them since they arrived, and when she did, she refused to meet Halloran's gaze.

After an eternity, Carver hung up the phone and made his way to the door of his office. He opened it slowly and nodded at the group in the foyer. "Gentlemen," he said coldly.

Halloran held up the paper. "Mayor, I have warrants to search your office, your vehicles, and your home with regards to the Sarah McElvoy case."

Carver's face turned ashen, and a muscle worked in his jaw. "I assumed that's why you were here," he said evenly. "You'll be glad to know I was on the phone with my attorney."

"That's a good idea," Halloran said. "Detective Chapman and I will be going over your office. Chief Pettus has another team at your home. You're welcome to wait out here with these officers. But we will need to ask you some more questions."

"You have no idea what you're dealing with," Carver spat. "I will own you."

"We just have some questions," Halloran said.

Carver looked at him hard. "I'm not answering *shit* until my attorney gets here. You're going to regret this."

Halloran shrugged. "Just make yourself comfortable for now."

5:38 PM

Joel was nervous as hell. A dull throb had begun behind his eyes, and he rubbed his temples to try to push it away.

He had planned on leaving at 5:30, but just now as he got a glimpse of himself in the bathroom mirror, he saw massive sweat stains on his shirt under the arms. In the bedroom, he ripped off the dirty shirt and fumbled through his closet for a clean one. He thought briefly of ironing it, but realized he wouldn't have time. Besides, it didn't look that bad.

God, he needed a cigarette. He'd smoked his last one at lunch, and he'd been jittery for the past hour. Whether it was from the lack of nicotine or his impending date, he wasn't sure. But he didn't want to meet Dana with cigarette breath.

He'd tried several times over the years to quit smoking. He'd used patches and gum, and once he'd even bought one of those electronic cigarettes off of television. Nothing had helped. The longest he'd been able to survive had been thirteen days last winter. That had been horrible. He had packed on ten pounds and had endured days of feeling as if he could crawl out of his skin and cling to the ceiling. By the time he gave in and finally had a smoke, his skin was sallow and his eyes were sunken in like a junkie's.

He fumbled with the pack on top of the bureau now, crinkling the cellophane on the box. He held it up to his face and breathed in the mellow aroma, feeling his pulse quicken as he did so. He tossed the cigarettes back where he found them. That would have to do.

On his way into town, he slowed down as he passed Wade's house. It looked like everyone was home. Joel wondered what kind of weird shit Wade had planned for the evening. He thought again of last Saturday, when Wade had been stoned and drinking. What kind of example was that for Derek? He remembered Marla calling him, teary and angry and. . . wounded. That was it. She had sounded wounded. It all made Joel's stomach burn. Wade didn't know how good he had it, and he was pissing it all away.

He thought of the night ahead of him, and the anger in his belly turned to panic. He hoped he didn't screw this up. Dana was the first girl that had shown any interest in him ever. And whether she was going tonight out of pity or because she genuinely liked him he didn't know. He didn't really care at this point. He just wanted to get through tonight and see what happened.

He pulled up to the address Dana had given him. It was a modest craftsman-style house with a wide front porch and a patriotic wreath on the door. The yard was immaculate, and a trellis of roses climbed to the second story. All very middle class.

Joel climbed out of the Explorer and made his way up the walk to the steps of the porch. There was a swing and a couple of wicker chairs, and he wondered if they all sat out here drinking lemonade and discussing the neighbors.

He rang the bell, and from behind the door came the sound of yapping. The door opened and Frank greeted him. He was a balding, pudgy man in his mid-fifties, much shorter than Joel, and his blue eyes were bright and friendly behind his glasses. "Hey, Joel." The dog, a Yorkie, continued to yap.

"Mr. West."

"Please. Call me Frank." The Yorkie was barking furiously at Joel. Frank nudged him with a sock-clad foot. "Shut up, George." The dog wandered off and Frank leaned in toward Joel. "I hate that dog," he whispered. "Come on in."

The living room was neat but not fussy. A newspaper was sprawled over the arm of the recliner and an old episode of *CSI: Miami* played on the ancient console television. A fireplace dominated one wall of the room, and Joel spotted a framed school picture of Dana sitting on the mantle. She appeared to be about twelve, though it was hard to say knowing she looked younger than her actual age.

Frank motioned to the couch. "Have a seat." He leaned through the doorway that led to the rest of the house and called for Dana, then sank back into the recliner. "So how're things going?" he said to Joel.

Joel nodded. "Good."

"What do you do again?"

"I work for the cable company. Service and installation."

Frank smirked. "Ah, so you're the one that bilks me out of ninety bucks every month and still can't keep the service from going out every time we have a thunderstorm." Joel felt his face flush, and Frank laughed. "Relax, I'm just kidding. I've been with the water department for thirty years, so I understand public disdain."

Joel laughed and felt himself loosening up. Frank seemed like an all-right guy. He leaned back into the couch and glanced at the TV screen. David Caruso was strutting around with his sunglasses in his hand, making some lame pun about a freshly-discovered body. Joel thought of his meeting with Halloran; he couldn't picture a detective from Cedar Hill parading around like an asshole. Halloran seemed like a man with more important things to do.

Frank picked up the newspaper and folded it, then picked up the remote and turned down the set. "I don't even like that show. I just keep the TV on for the noise."

"Hey, Joel."

Joel looked up to see Dana in the doorway. She was wearing a gray silk top with a blue paisley pattern and a pair of jeans, and her face was bright and flushed. He wanted to tell her how wonderful she looked, how the sight of her made his heart feel like a small bird trapped in his chest, how he was suddenly light-headed and exhilarated. Instead, he stood and managed to choke out, "Hey."

"So where we going?" she asked. "I'm starved."

"You like Chinese?"

"My favorite!" She leaned over and gave Frank a kiss on his bald spot. "See ya later, Daddy."

Frank had unfolded the newspaper and spread it out on his lap. "Have fun, you two."

8:48 PM

"Holy shit," Halloran said.

Three police cruisers plus the Chief's unmarked sedan were parked in the mayor's driveway. The windows of the house blazed with light, as if a grand party were going on inside. Halloran counted three officers milling around the front door, which meant there were at least three more inside, plus the two behind Halloran's car bringing home the mayor. If a criminal wanted to strike somewhere in Cedar Hill, tonight was the time.

They had found nothing in Carver's office. He and Chapman had combed through every drawer, every cabinet, every niche. They had looked in every file, had thumbed through every paper, had looked at every entry in Carver's calendar. Nothing. Not even any cryptic notes. The state crime lab had hauled off Carver's computer, but there would be no word on that until at least the middle of next week.

Likewise, Carver's Navigator had come up clean. No stray hairs or visible bodily fluids anywhere. Even running a blacklight over the interior of the vehicle failed to come up with anything.

"I hope we've got something here at the house," Chapman said.

Halloran grunted. The last thing the department needed was to come up empty after this circus. He and Chapman would both be lucky to have jobs.

He parked behind the chief's car and watched as the mayor climbed out of the police cruiser behind. Carver was red-faced and exuded anger like heat waves. Halloran met his gaze but didn't let his face betray the turmoil he was feeling in his gut.

Officer Brooks met Halloran and Chapman at the front door. "Lieutenant, the Chief wants to see you in the basement."

A spark of hope lit up Halloran's chest. "Have we got something?"

Brooks shrugged. "Not sure." He led the detectives through the massive living room down a short hallway to an open door. Brooks point toward the door. "He's down there."

Halloran ducked down the narrow stairs into the jumbled basement. He heard Chapman blow out a breath behind him and suppressed a grin; he knew Chapman hated tight spaces.

"Halloran!" The chief waved them over to a dark corner. "What'd you find at the office?"

"Nothing," Halloran said. "The office and the vehicle are as clean as a whistle. You find anything here?"

Pettus grunted and gave him a hard look, then shined his flashlight down at a pile of newspapers in the seat of a straight-back chair. "Here are the clippings."

Halloran leafed through them, reading the headlines. "Just like Joel Roberts said." He looked at the top one, at the fuzzy photograph of Carmelita Santos, and felt a shiver as he remembered their visit to give the family the bad news. He dropped the pile back into the chair. "Anything else?"

"Just this."

Pettus reached behind him and swung open a section of the paneled wall, revealing the sex sling suspended from the ceiling in the vinyl-covered room behind. Halloran squinted against the maddening flicker of the strobe light. "Lab guys were here and took some swabs off the floor and walls, but I can tell you what they found wasn't blood."

Halloran gave a humorless chuckle. "So the mayor and his wife are a little kinky."

Pettus shook his head. "Evidently not. We talked to Mrs. Carver. She had no idea the room was even here."

"You're kidding."

"Nope. She was as surprised as your man probably was when he stumbled over it."

"Interesting."

Pettus closed the door and looked at Halloran. "Look, I want to catch this perp as much as anyone, but I'm beginning to think this lead is as good as dead. All we've managed to do so far is piss off the man in charge."

"There's got to be more," Halloran said. "This can't be all."

Pettus lowered his voice to a whisper. "You'd better hope so. Otherwise the whole goddamned department's going to be looking for work." He left them and made his way up the stairs.

Halloran blew out a breath. It was going to be a long night.

SATURDAY, JULY 14

7:47 AM

Joel came awake slowly as the early morning sunlight peeked in through the crack in the blinds. He rolled over and looked at the clock, then started to reach for the cigarettes. He stopped himself and lay back down but continued to stare at the pack. He hadn't given in even after he got home last night, even though he had been dying for a smoke. But something about being with Dana had made his willpower stronger. He wondered if it was love.

Dinner had been great. They talked over their meal as if they had known each other all their lives. Dana told him all about growing up with her gift, how many of her schoolmates had avoided her out of fear or mistrust, how she had felt like a freak most of her life, how she hadn't really begun to find herself until after graduation when she entered college. "That's when I found the group," she said, "I knew I wasn't alone. It was the best feeling in the world."

"But what about your parents?" Joel said. "They had the same gift as you."

Dana shook her head. "You don't understand. I wanted *friends*. People my own age to run around with. I didn't want to go stale sitting at home every night with my parents."

"That makes sense."

"Getting involved with the group gave me the self-confidence to try new things and meet new people. I was able to stop focusing on my abilities and actually live for a change."

Joel looked at her across the table and thought she was the most remarkable human being he had ever met. He found himself suddenly wanting to lean across and kiss her, to feel her moist lips press against his, to explore her mouth with the tip of his tongue. It was a feeling that lasted all through the meal and continued to course through him as they sat in the darkened theater watching an Andy Samberg comedy. Listening to her laugh was like hearing a jazz combo playing a light, lilting tune you knew you would never get out of your head. Again, he wondered what he would see if he reached over and took her hand, but she caught him staring at her and gave him a quick smile before turning back to the screen. And later, as he dropped her back home and she thanked him for the evening, she brushed her lips against his cheek—just softly and quickly enough that all he read off of her was that she was happy. And that was enough.

And now he lay in the bed wondering what would have happened if he had just wrapped his arms around her and kissed her like he wanted. Would he have fallen into pure ecstasy at the touch of her lips? Or would the sensation have been too much? Just like—

Did you know there were canals on Mars?

Just like that night long ago.

Hey, Roberts!

And before he could stop himself, he was back there on that crisp October evening a decade ago. Friday night after the football game. Cruising around with Mike Bennett and Scott Harris in Mike's T-Bird. Drinking Bud Light and blasting Nelly. All stoked up because they had won their game and now they were going to celebrate and have some fun and maybe tear some shit up. And Joel didn't care because at least he would be out of the house and not having to take a bunch of grief from Clifton. And maybe he could forget about these weird sensations he was having every time he made contact with someone on the football field, as if he was seeing inside them, feeling inside them. How brushing against someone was like hearing fifty radios blasting at him all at once.

And when they caught up to Candy Johnson walking along Eighth Street, he was more than happy to scoot over and share the backseat with her, to pull a bottle from the second six-pack of the night and hand it to her. And how he had watched—fascinated—as she turned up the bottle and drank it down in four gulps and asked for another.

And soon he and Candy were talking about school

and Mr. Peterson's astronomy class and he said, "Did you know there were canals on Mars?"

"Really?" she asked and took a sip of beer.

He wasn't sure if she was actually interested or she was just zoning out from the beer, but he said, "Yeah. A long time ago they thought that meant there was water there. And life."

"Real Martians?"

"Yeah."

A little while later they were parked at a clearing out by the railroad tracks, and Joel and Scott sat draining the last of the beer while Mike and Candy were getting busy in the back seat. And it wasn't long before Mike crawled out, zipping up his jeans, and said, "Hey, Roberts! She wants you now," and Scott clapped Joel on the back and shoved him toward the car.

And suddenly Joel was standing at the open door of the T-Bird, staring in at the darkness where he could just see Candy lying in the backseat illuminated by the lights from the dashboard. Usher was pounding in the speakers, and Joel could feel the throb of the bass course through his chest, down through his belly to his cock, which strained against the fly of his jeans. And all he could think, even through the fog of the beer buzz, was that it all seemed wrong somehow, that a few minutes ago they were discussing Mars and now she was fucking them all and it was dirty and wrong but he still wanted to do it because this would be the first time he had ever had sex with anyone besides his own hand. And immediately he ripped open his jeans and knelt between her legs and plunged into the slickness and felt her arch up to meet him.

And that was when all the sensations hit him. A roar of sounds and a dizzying array of visions pierced through him. He saw Candy with a dozen other guys. Felt the emptiness that was her soul. Saw her whole filthy, stinking squalid existence in a matter of seconds. He managed to pull away from her and stumble back out of the car, his erection wilted and his pants still wrapped around his knees. His body was coated with sweat, and he realized tears were streaming down his face.

"That was quick," Mike said, laughing.

Scott moved toward the car and threw his empty beer bottle into the woods. "My turn," he said.

Joel hadn't been with anyone since. The thought of being pummeled by that cacophony of energy and emotion again was more than he could bear. He had quit football not long after that, and when he understood the weight of his ability he began to shut himself off from other people. Sex had not been something he had wanted to repeat.

But now he found himself thinking of Dana and how much he enjoyed being with her, and he wondered if she felt the same. And would she still want him if she knew they could never be together physically?

His phone buzzed on the table beside him, startling him out of his thoughts. He grabbed it and looked at the number, hoping it would be Dana. But it was a number he didn't recognize. Against his better judgment, he accepted the call. "Hello?"

"Is this Joel?" said a male voice.

"Yes. Who's this?"

"This is Barry. From the group."

Joel remembered him. The creepy red-haired guy. "Hi, Barry."

"Listen, I'm really sorry to bother you, and I hope you don't mind me calling you, but I need to tell you something."

"Yes?"

"I think you're in danger."

Joel sat up in the bed. "What?"

"I think something may happen to you. Something bad."

A cold sweat had broken out on Joel's forehead. "Like what?"

"I'm not sure. I don't want to alarm you, I. . . just think you should be careful."

Joel stared straight ahead at the blinds over the window. His skin prickled and he realized he had goosebumps down his arms.

"Joel, you there?"

"I'm here."

"Tackle him. Even if you think it's too dangerous. Do it anyway. You'll know when." He disconnected and Joel sat with the dead phone against his ear, listening to the silence.

10:35 AM

Wade watched Derek work the lug nuts on the wheel of the Mustang. Today he was going to replace the brakes and hopefully take the car out for a spin when he was done. It was already sweltering in the barn, even though he had propped the doors and windows open and a breeze was flowing through like a hot river. He wiped the sweat off his face with the tail of his t-shirt and leaned back against the workbench.

"Think you'll be done by the time I get home from work?" Derek said.

"Should be."

"I'd like to take Chad for a ride. I've been telling him about it and he really wants to see it."

"As long as you don't do any drinking."

Derek blew out a breath. "We won't."

"I don't want to have to bail you outa jail."

Derek shook his head. "Why are you always saying that?"

Wade grunted. "Hey, I was sixteen once."

"Was alcohol even invented yet when you were sixteen?"

Wade picked up a rusty washer and chucked it at the kid's ear. "Watch it."

Derek stood up and stretched, then looked at his watch. "Crap, I gotta get to work." He tossed the lug wrench to Wade. "If I'm late again, I'll get an ass-chewing." He cracked his neck and headed out into the yard. "See ya."

"Have a great day at the office," Wade called.

"Yeah."

Wade watched him make his way up the back steps into the house, and a couple of minutes later heard the Escort fire up and pull out onto the highway with a squeal of tires. When he was sure he was alone and that Marla wasn't going to make an appearance, he pulled the cigar box from the notch in the wall and rolled up a joint. He fired it up and sat down in the old chair, watching the leaves rustle in the trees outside.

Last night had been a strange one. He had fully intended to clean up after work and head into town, to cruise by the Capitol and meet up with Shelley and Abby again. But neither Marla nor Derek was home when he got there. The pickup was gone, and there was no sign of dinner. He sat down on the couch to wait for one of them to pull into the drive and fell asleep watching the news. When he awoke, it was almost eleven, Derek was coming through the front door smelling like old grease and hamburgers, and Marla was still gone. He ate a bowl of Frosted Flakes and sat stupidly looking at the television, his head thick and groggy.

And when Marla came through the door a few minutes later, looking disheveled and flustered, he simply looked at her and said, "Where the fuck have you been?"

She averted her gaze from him and walked through the room toward the stairs. "I went to the movies."

"Alone?"

She stared back at him this time, meeting his eyes. "Yes. Then I went and got something to eat."

He felt rage building up in his gut. "You think I believe that?"

A muscle was working in her jaw. "I don't care what you believe." She tromped on upstairs, and Wade heard her moving around in the bedroom, then the sound of the shower.

He sat there, still looking at the television screen, wondering if she had been out with another man and why he didn't just get up and beat the shit out of her. But in the end he decided he was just too damned tired. The last weekend of partying seemed to have caught up with him, and all he wanted to do was rest. And besides, even if Marla was seeing someone, he really didn't give a fuck anymore. He flipped off the TV and made his way upstairs and collapsed next to her in the bed.

And now as he sat in the dry heat of the barn and watched the shadows of the trees play across the green grass outside, he took another hit off the joint and thought of what he would do if Marla was cheating. In the end he figured it might be for the best. He would be free to do whatever the hell he wanted.

Wade smiled and felt his body melt into the chair. He would finish the joint and then get started on the brakes. And later he might head into town and try to meet up with the girls.

The day stretched lazily before him, full of fun and promise.

1:15 PM

Halloran stared at the remaining fries on his plate and took another sip of his Coke. He and Chapman had met for lunch at a small diner near the police station to talk about what their next move would be. He hoped it wouldn't involve looking for a new job.

Last night had not gone well. Other than the clippings and the sex sling in the basement, the search of the mayor's house had turned up nothing. Larry Carver was pissed. Chief Pettus was pissed. Hell, Halloran was pissed himself. Something wasn't adding up. He was missing something, he knew it.

"You gonna eat those?" Chapman asked, pointing to Halloran's fries.

Halloran grunted and slid the plate across the table. He watched Chapman shove the fries into his mouth and for a split second felt a shiver of revulsion. He licked his dry lips. He really needed a cigarette, but since the city passed the smoking ban last March he would have to wait until he got out to the car before lighting up. "You've certainly got a healthy appetite," Halloran said.

Chapman licked his fingers. "I eat when I'm nervous. Especially when I'm about to be on the unemployment line."

"Nobody's going to be on the unemployment line," Halloran said, and hoped he sounded convincing. "Besides, who're they going to get to do our jobs?"

"Brooks would make a good detective," Chapman said.

Halloran nodded. "I've thought the same thing myself. He doesn't have the experience yet, though."

"Or the training."

Halloran blew out a breath. "I just knew we'd find something at Carver's house. I felt it."

Chapman popped the last fry into his mouth. "Maybe the lab will come up with something off those swabs."

"Maybe." Halloran sipped his Coke. "In the mean-time, we'll just stay out of Carver's way. It'll all blow over eventually."

* * *

A little after seven, just as Halloran had settled in to watch the Cardinals game, he was summoned to an apartment building on Woodside. Chapman was already there, along with a couple of other officers.

One of the cops met him at the door, an obnoxious little guy named Pavoni. "Missing girl is Abigail Saunders," Pavoni said, reading off his notepad. "Roommate said she hadn't been able to reach her cell all weekend. Came in and found the place a mess about a half hour ago. Parents haven't heard from her either."

Halloran glanced at the sofa, where a sobbing blonde was already talking to Chapman.

"Back bedroom looks like a tornado went through it," Pavoni went on. "Roommate was out of town last night, so we think that's probably when it happened."

Halloran peered into the hallway beyond. "Any crime techs here?"

Pavoni shook his head and jerked a thumb behind him. "Go on back."

Halloran slipped past him and stuck his head in the doorway. The place was completely trashed. Clothing and books littered the floor. An overturned lamp by the bed cast grotesque shadows on the ceiling. He turned and made his way back to the living room and found Pavoni. "Anyone hear anything?"

"Nothing," Pavoni told him. "All the tenants were out last night, and the old lady downstairs in the corner unit couldn't hear thunder."

"Anything missing?"

"The roommate hasn't noticed anything gone, but with the mess, who knows." Pavoni thumbed through his notes. "Oh, here's something that might interest you. One of the neighbors noticed a black Ford Escort hanging around a good part of the morning yesterday. He said there was a guy inside, but he couldn't get a good look at him. We've got an ATL out on the vehicle now."

"Good." Halloran pulled out his own notepad and jotted the information down. "I'll check further on that."

The roommate had finished talking to Chapman and was heading out the front door with a female officer. Chapman made his way over to Halloran. "It's a mess back there."

Halloran nodded. "Get anywhere with the roommate?"

"Not really. She's gonna spend the night with a friend and come down to talk to us in the morning."

Halloran blew out a breath. "Jesus, what else can happen in this town?"

8:43 PM

Wade had been sitting in the Capitol for almost half an hour now and Shelley and Abby were nowhere to be seen. He was still nursing his first beer at one of the side tables where he could keep an eye on the entrance to the club, and although quite a few hot women had come in, none of them were in the same league as his girls. He laughed at that. "His girls." It made him sound like a pimp.

He wondered, not for the first time, if Shelley and Abby had just been playing him, fucking with him. Perhaps they were tired of him already. They had all had some fun, but now maybe that was over. It would be no less than he deserved. He glanced at his watch again. It was still early, they still might show.

But finally at a quarter to nine, just as the crowd was becoming unbearably close, he decided he'd had enough. He had left his phone back at the house, so he couldn't call them. They weren't coming, and since this really wasn't his scene, he figured he would head over to the Wild Horse and see what was happening there.

He pulled his truck out of the parking lot and on a whim swung a right and headed back toward the college campus. Maybe he would just drive by the house and see if anything was going on. Maybe they were entertaining some other man. Maybe he would surprise them. Maybe they would ask him to join them.

He turned onto Woodside and came to a screeching halt. There was something going on, all right. Three police cars and an ambulance were parked out front. The entire neighborhood was bathed in whirling, flashing light, and several people milled about in the street and on the sidewalk.

His breath had left his body and a cold sweat trickled down his forehead. What the fuck? He had no idea what to think. What had happened? Were they all right? Was someone hurt? He sat there, looking at the activity surrounding the apartment house, feeling a cold dread pulse through him.

Something banged on the hood of the truck and he looked up to see a stout cop waving him on. "Come on, buddy, you can't come this way."

Wade nodded and waved back. He turned down a side street and headed back toward the edge of town, toward the Wild Horse. Behind him, the lights continued to flash with sickening intensity.

11:32 PM

He drove through the darkened town away from the campus, weaving through the traffic. Even for Saturday night there seemed to be more people out than usual. But no one was paying him any attention. His car was plain and unobtrusive. He had planned it that way.

It was going to be so easy to connect the missing girl with the others. Those stupid fucking assholes couldn't see past the ends of their dicks. When he was finished, they would tie all the girls together and then he would be home free. It couldn't have been any better if he had planned it this way. It was as if all the stars had aligned or something.

He had just left the shopping district, heading toward the residential area, when he saw her. She plodded along the sidewalk in shorts and flipflops. A backpack in the form of a purple stuffed monkey hung over her shoulders beneath long tresses of blond hair. She turned toward him and the headlights brushed her face. She looked a little older—maybe fifteen—but she was unblemished and perfect.

He slowed down to match her gait and lowered the passenger side window. "Hey," he said. "You're out kinda late."

"Heading home," she said. "I'm gonna catch it for being out past eleven."

He cleared his throat. "Need a ride?"

She looked up and down the deserted street, then smiled at him. He felt the blood rush to his crotch. She wasn't afraid of him. They never were.

SUNDAY, JULY 15

10:45 AM

For the first time since the search at his home, Halloran found himself face to face with Larry Carver.

Halloran and Pettus sat on one side of the table in the interrogation room and Carver and his attorney sat on the other. Carver's face was stony and red and his cold eyes darted between Halloran and the chief. If Halloran had had any doubts about how pissed off Carver was, they were gone now. The man exuded anger like an odor. Carver's lawyer, a well-respected attorney by the name of Daniel Woods, looked equally pissed. He wore the expression of someone who had just stepped on a disgusting insect.

"I suppose you're wondering why we called you in here," Halloran said.

Carver's nostrils flared. "I would have thought Friday night would have been the end of it, when you didn't find anything."

Woods laid a pudgy hand on the mayor's arm. "Easy, Larry."

Halloran opened the file folder in front of him and pulled out an eight-by-ten photo. Wordlessly he slid it across the desk to the other two men.

Carver looked at it, then blew out a breath. "I give up. What the hell am I supposed to be looking at?"

"Tire track," Halloran said. "We found this on the river bank near where the McElvoy and the Santos girl both washed up."

"So?"

Halloran pulled out a second photograph and laid it beside the first. "This is the front passenger tire on your Lincoln Navigator. It's a perfect match. Right down to a piece of gravel stuck in the tread." He pointed with the end of an ink pen. "Here."

Carver slammed a fist down on the table. "I had nothing to do with those girls," he spat.

Woods put a hand on Carver's shoulder. "Don't say anything else, Larry."

Carver shrugged out from under Woods' grip. "Get your goddamned hand off me."

"Are you denying this track is off your vehicle?" Pettus asked.

"I know it's mine," Carver said, and Halloran felt a thrill through his gut.

Woods' face was ashen. "Larry. . ."

"Shut up," Carver told him. "These people want some dirt on the mayor, and they'll get some dirt on the mayor." Carver swallowed and looked at Halloran. "I was at the river. I won't deny it. I've been there several times over the past few weeks."

"Doing what exactly?" Halloran asked.

Carver shifted in his seat. "I've been down there with a few. . . ladies."

Pettus gaped at the mayor. "You mean, hookers?"

Carver nodded and stared at the table. "Hookers, prostitutes. . . whatever you want to call them. I usually pick them up on Fourth Street." He looked at Pettus. "You know where I'm talking about."

Pettus nodded. "But why take them down there?"

"So we won't be seen," Carver said. "I can't very well risk checking into a motel in town, now can I?"

"Can any of these women verify your story?" Halloran asked.

"Undoubtedly." Carver rattled off three or four names, including one well-known transvestite. Halloran shot a glance at Pettus and saw just the faintest trace of a smile play across his lips.

There was a knock at the door, and Chapman stuck his head in and motioned for Halloran to join him in the hallway. Halloran excused himself and slipped out the door.

"How's it going in there?" Chapman asked.

Halloran shook his head. "He didn't do it."

"What about the track?"

Halloran told him what Carver had divulged, and they shared a quiet snicker over the transvestite.

"You think he knew it was really a guy?" Chapman asked.

Halloran chuckled. "After what we found in his

basement I wouldn't be surprised." His gaze fell on the papers in Chapman's hand. "What's up?"

"Been talking with Shelley Mitchell—the roommate of the Saunders girl."

"What'd you find out?"

Chapman glanced at his notes. "We've got a person of interest. She says the two of them partied a couple of times with a guy named Wade Roberts."

Roberts. That name sounded familiar. "Wasn't the guy that came in to see me about the mayor named Roberts? Didn't he say he had a brother named Wade?"

Chapman nodded. "One and the same."

Halloran looked away, thinking.

"Oh, and get this," Chapman said. "I ran a search on all the vehicles registered in Wade Roberts' name. Got a hit on a black Ford Escort like the kind that was seen in the Saunders girl's neighborhood."

Halloran took a deep breath. "Sounds like we need to pay a visit to Mr. Wade Roberts."

11:30 AM

Derek sat at his desk watching as the homepage for *hotbabes.com* loaded with agonizing slowness on his computer screen. Fucking dial-up internet. As close as they were to town they should at least be able to get DSL. Chad's house had cable internet and they could watch full porn movies there. But here he was stuck with stills and most of them low-resolution. Hell, his dick would be limp by the time he got to see his first tit.

The crunch of gravel out in the driveway startled him. That couldn't be his mom. It was too early for her to be home from church. He glanced out his window to see an unmarked sedan pulling in. The car stopped and two men in suits climbed out. One was a red-headed guy with freckles. The other had dark hair and a mustache, and Derek thought he may have seen him on the news. What the fuck were they doing here?

He slipped out of his room and padded barefoot to the top of the stairs. Below through the frosted glass of the front door he watched them step up onto the porch. There was a second of silence, and then a light knock. Wade had heard them as well, and he was already at the door to meet them.

"Mr. Roberts?" came a voice on the other side.

"Yeah?"

"I'm Lieutenant Mike Halloran and this is my partner John Chapman. We'd like to ask you a few questions if you have a few minutes."

Wade stepped back and opened the door wide. "Sure, come on in."

The other men stepped into the living room and the one with the mustache looked up and locked glances with Derek. He nodded in greeting and Derek nodded back.

Wade motioned to the couch. "Have a seat."

The three of them had moved out of Derek's field of vision, but he heard Wade say, "What's this all about?"

One of the cops said, "We're investigating the disappearance of a female college student. Abigail Saunders. She hasn't been seen since Friday night."

"What's this got to do with me?"

The other man said, "Do you own a 2003 Ford Escort?"

"That's my son's car.

Derek felt sweat pop out on his brow. *Fuck, oh fuck.*

"That car was seen hanging around the Saunders girl's apartment on Friday."

"What?" his father said.

"Is your son here?" the first cop asked. "Maybe we can clear all this up."

"Derek!" his father called, and Derek's legs suddenly felt like rubber.

He moved down the stairs to the living room. The two detectives were sitting on the couch. Wade sat in his recliner. They were all looking at him. "Sit," Wade told him. Derek sank into the chair closest to the cops.

The one with the mustache said, "Were you hanging around on Woodside Avenue on Friday?"

Derek shot a glance at his father, then looked at the floor. There was no reason to lie about it. They already knew it was him. "Yeah, I was there."

"What were you doing?"

"Following a girl."

The detective pulled out a small photograph and showed it to him. It was the angel. "This her?"

Derek nodded. "That's her."

"Why were you following her?"

Derek looked at him. "I thought she was pretty. I just wanted to see where she lived, what she was doing."

"How many times had you been there?"

"Just twice. I followed her home from the Gas-N-Pack on Thursday."

"And you went back there on Friday?" the other detective asked.

Derek nodded. "I know it was stupid. I just wanted to get a look at her again."

"Did you?"

Panic was starting to boil in Derek's stomach. "Yeah. I followed her back to the college. I asked her out, but she kinda blew me off."

"That make you mad?" the cop with the mustache asked.

"Sort of."

"Then what happened?"

Derek looked at him. "Nothing. I came back home."

"Did you go back to her apartment?"

"No," Derek said, "I told you I came back home."

"You're sure you didn't go back?"

Beside him, Wade sat up on the edge of his chair. "Look, he said he didn't go back there. What's going on?"

The detective with the mustache looked at Wade. "Look, Mr. Roberts, we know you're acquainted with Miss Saunders. We talked to her roommate."

Derek watched his father's face grow red, then purple. He thought at first Wade was having a stroke. "Dad. . . ?"

Wade looked at him, then back at the cop. He licked his lips. "Yes, I know them. We partied together a few times."

"So we've been told." The cop looked at Wade squarely. "Look, Mr. Roberts, Abigail Saunders hasn't been seen since Shelley Mitchell left their apartment on Friday at four o'clock. We're suspecting foul play."

Wade shot a glance at Derek. "And you think one of *us* had something to do with it?"

"That's what we're trying to find out." He shifted in his seat. "Look, we know you both know her. Maybe you found out she had a thing for your son and it made you mad."

Honestly, now Wade's head looked like it was going to explode. Sweat was pouring down his face. "I think we're done here," he said, and Derek could tell it was taking everything Wade had to stay calm. "We're not answering anything else."

The detective shrugged. "Suit yourself." He and the other man stood, and Wade did the same. "We'll be back."

"You better have a warrant."

"We will."

The two men went out the front door. Wade followed them and watched them get back into their car. He whispered, "Fuck."

Derek watched the car back out of the driveway and then looked back at Wade. "Dad? What's going on?"

Wade kept his gaze on the black sedan. "Nothing. Not a goddamned thing." When the car was out of sight, Wade shut the door and looked at him. "Not one word about this to your mother. Understand? Not one fucking word."

"Do you really know that girl?"

Wade didn't answer him. He sat back down the recliner and turned on the television. The NASCAR race was just starting and Wade stared at it without saying anything else.

Derek turned and headed back up the stairs. Something weird was happening. Something weird and big.

2:10 PM

For mid-July the day had turned out breezy and pleasant. The humidity of the past week was gone, and that made the heat easier to tolerate. Joel was glad. He was always miserable to the point of exhaustion in the heat. And today he did not want to be miserable.

He and Dana had come to Riverside Park for the afternoon. Dana had packed a picnic lunch for them—"Cheesy, I know," she told him with an embarrassed laugh—and they had enjoyed it in the shade of the tall oaks by the river. The breeze coming over the water was steady and almost cool. Joel tilted his head back and breathed in the fresh air. It was hard to believe this area had been swarming with cops just a few days ago.

"It was right down there where they found those bodies, wasn't it?" Dana said, making him jump.

"You sure you don't read minds?" Joel said and gave her a grin. He pointed to a pile of brush at the water's edge. "There, where all those limbs and branches are."

Dana shivered. "I still can't believe it happened here in Cedar Hill."

"I can't believe they haven't caught the guy yet."

"Wonder if you and I could solve it?" she said. "Between the two of us, reading people and objects, I bet we could find him in no time flat."

"Maybe." He hadn't yet told her about his visit with Lieutenant Halloran, and he wondered if they had even followed up on his lead with the mayor. He had been watching the news every night since, but there had been no mention of anything. Just as well. He was sure he had come across as some kind of nut case, and if he presented himself as a psychic that would certainly seal it for him. "You ever work with the police?"

"No, but I see it all the time on TV."

Joel grunted. "Something tells me our local cops wouldn't be as generous with their time."

"Maybe not." She took a deep breath and blew it out. "I'd just like to help some way, you know?"

Joel nodded. He thought of the mothers he had seen on the news and their tearful, desperate pleas and how he wished to be able to either find their children or bring them some closure. He stared out across the river. "I went to the police last week," he said.

She gaped at him. "What? Why?"

He told her everything about what he found in the mayor's house, about speaking with Halloran and how he came away feeling he might have done more harm than good.

"But you were just doing what you felt you had to," Dana said. "I would have done the same thing."

He smiled at her. "I know you would."

"And you don't know what may be going on with the investigation that isn't being made public." Her voice was sounding excited, and it was cute in a way.

"Maybe they're watching the mayor, seeing what his next move is. Maybe they're on a stakeout at his house."

Joel thought of the detectives he had talked to sitting in a darkened sedan with coffee and donuts and had to laugh.

Dana looked at him. "What?"

He shook his head. "You're hilarious." He opened his mouth to tell her about the strange call from Barry, but he stopped himself. He wasn't sure he wanted to get into that right now.

Dana smiled and pulled a dandelion from the grass and twirled it in her fingers. He watched her and felt a strange warmth surge through him. And he knew what it was.

He was falling in love.

4:45 PM

Halloran could tell Wade Roberts was not surprised to see him again. Even as patrol cars swarmed into the driveway while he was serving the warrant, Roberts showed no emotion. Behind him, Halloran saw a haggard blonde woman—presumably his wife—peeking at them from the kitchen.

"This is bullshit, you know," Roberts told him.

"Maybe it is," Halloran said.

Roberts, his wife, and his son waited outside on the lawn while several men entered the house with Pettus. Chapman and another cop took the vehicles, and Halloran headed toward the barn and outbuildings with

Brooks.

Inside the barn was a vehicle beneath a stained tarp. Halloran pulled the tarp off and Brooks whistled softly.

It was a Mustang. A 'sixty-four-and-a-half or a 'sixty-five from the looks of it. It appeared Roberts was in the process of restoring it.

"Nice car," Brooks said. "I always wanted a Mustang."

"I had one," Halloran told him. "A 'sixty-seven."

"No shit?"

"Damn thing was always breaking down. It was in the shop more than it was on the road." He ran his fingertips along the ridge of the front fender. "They're nice when they're fully restored, but unless you got a boatload of money to sink into one, they're more trouble than they're worth."

"You still have yours?"

"Nah. Sold it a year or two after I bought it. I was fresh out of college and struggling to make it to my next paycheck. I couldn't afford to work on my car all the time."

"That's a shame."

Halloran stared at the car. "Yeah, it is." He opened the door. "Might as well start here."

But the Mustang came up clean, and he and Brooks turned their attention to the boxes and crates stored around it. There appeared to be nothing here but tools and rusted paint cans.

Halloran had just shoved a cardboard box back under the workbench when he spotted something stuck behind one of the wall studs. He reached for it and pulled out a worn cigar box. Inside was a small bag of marijuana and some rolling papers. "Well, well, well," he said. He held up the bag for Brooks to see.

"If nothing else, we got him on possession," Brooks said.

Halloran set the box and its contents on the hood of the car and pulled out his digital camera to get a shot of it.

"Lieutenant?"

Halloran looked up to see one of the younger officers at the door of the barn. "Yes?"

"Detective Chapman sent me to get you. He says there's something you need to take a look at."

Halloran snapped the picture and pointed to Brooks. "Get that tagged and bagged." He followed the younger officer outside. "Find something in the Escort?"

The cop shook his head. "Kid's car was clean. Got something in the dad's truck."

Several officers and Chapman were huddled around the passenger side of blue Ford pickup. Halloran came up behind them and laid a hand on Chapman's shoulder. "What's up?"

Chapman turned and held up something in his gloved fingers. It was Abigail Saunders' driver's license. "It was under the passenger seat," he said. "Just laying there."

"Get it bagged," Halloran said.

"There's something else," Chapman said. He lifted his other hand. He was holding a pair of tweezers, and when Halloran saw what was in them he felt his knees go weak.

"I'll be goddamned," he said.

5:42 PM

It had been a damn fine day, Joel thought.

He and Dana had spent the remainder of the after-noon walking through the park and talking. Dana had chatted on and on about the murders like she was dis-cussing a mystery novel. And while her enthusiasm and her wanting to help out were charming and energiz-ing, Joel had been glad when the conversation had turned to something else.

They talked about their futures. Dana would gradu-ate college next spring and hoped to become an elementary teacher. Joel could see her doing that. She was so much like a child herself—full of imagination and life. Little kids would love her. But as much as he enjoyed hearing her hopes and plans, he couldn't help but feel a spark of jealousy. She knew what she wanted out of life. She knew where she was going. All he would ever be was a lowly peon, doomed to an endless dead-end job until he was worn down and able to draw his retirement.

But maybe with the right woman to spend the rest of his life with, it would be all right. Maybe the banality of life would be easier to take. Maybe Dana was that woman. He smiled to himself. Maybe she was the an-swer he had been searching for.

He still didn't know why he hadn't told her about Barry's call, but he knew she would worry, and worry-ing Dana was not something he wanted to do. He smiled at that. Having a woman worry over him was not something he was used to.

He had just turned the corner below Wade's house when the flashing lights caught his attention. Lots of them. He slowed the Explorer down to a crawl as panic filled his gut. Cop cars all over Wade's lawn. What the hell was going on? Was someone hurt?

Then he spotted them—Wade, Marla and Derek— standing beside one of the cop cars. Wade was smoking a cigarette. Marla's face was puffy, as if she'd been crying. Derek wore a fuck-all expression, like he had been mightily inconvenienced.

Joel turned into the drive and a heavily muscled cop raised a hand to stop him. "You can't come in here," he shouted.

Joel lowered the window. "This is my brother's house. Is everything okay?"

The cop looked around behind him, then back at Joel. "Everything's under control. Everybody's all right."

"Can I see him?"

The cop looked around again, then nodded. "Park over there out of the way," he said, motioning to an empty area close to the road.

Joel pulled the Explorer over and climbed out, then threaded his way through the maze of lights and cars to where the three of them stood.

Wade spotted him first, and his face changed from indifference, to annoyance, to relief in a matter of seconds. "What are you doing here?"

"What's going on?" Joel asked. "Is everything okay?"

"Some girl's disappeared," Wade said flatly. "They think me or Derek had something to do with it."

"What? Who?"

Wade looked at him for a moment, then dropped his gaze to the ground. "Just a girl I know, okay?"

Joel glanced at Marla and saw fresh tears welling up in her eyes. She stared straight ahead as if she could wish herself out of here.

"They think she's dead," Derek said.

Joel looked at him and saw that what he had first thought was an expression of defiance was actually fear. The boy's hands were trembling and Joel could see he had bitten off most of his fingernails.

Wade dropped his cigarette butt and ground it into the dirt with the heel of his boot. "Fucking cops. I didn't have anything to do with this. Derek didn't have anything to do with it. This is all a bunch of bullshit."

Joel stared at Wade. He knew Wade had been involved in some heavy shit over the years, and he also knew Wade had been partying more than usual lately. But could he actually be involved in something else?

There was one way to know, and even though Joel didn't want to do it, he knew he had to. He moved over to Wade and leaned against the car beside him. "Everything will be okay," he said. Then he placed his hand on Wade's shoulder in a display of brotherly concern.

As many times as he had done this, he was still unprepared each time for the waves of sensations that tore through him. He saw it all, felt it all. He saw the end-

less stream of women, saw the barely-contained violence toward Marla, saw the drugs and booze and sex.
Felt the claustrophobic existence of home and family.
And he saw with sickening clarity what Clifton had
done to him all those years ago. But there was nothing
at all to indicate Wade had been involved in anyone's
disappearance. Wade was a partier and an adulterer,
but he was not a killer.

Joel let go and slumped against the car. He was
drained. For a moment he thought his legs would give
out and he would tumble to the ground, but he managed
to brace himself against the hood of the Crown Victo-
ria.

Wade looked at him. "You okay?"

Joel nodded. "Just tired."

"Mr. Roberts?"

Coming across the yard was the detective Joel had
spoken with last week, Halloran. He was with a younger lanky man in a white dress shirt and tie, presumably
another detective, and a stocky police officer. Halloran
met Joel's gaze, and Joel noticed the flash of recogni-
tion in his eyes. He nodded and Joel nodded back. But
now he realized Halloran had been addressing Wade.

Wade stood up straight.

"Mr. Roberts, I'm gonna need you to turn around,"
the stocky cop said.

"Wait," said Wade, "what?"

"Turn around and place your hands behind your
back."

Wade's eyes grew round with fear and anger. "What
is this?"

"We found your stash in the barn," Halloran said. "We're taking you in for possession of marijuana and drug paraphernalia. We're also placing you under arrest in the disappearance of Abigail Saunders."

"What the *fuck?*" Wade cried. "I didn't do anything!"

"We found Miss Saunders' license in your truck," Halloran said.

"That's impossible," Wade said.

Joel could only stand there as the burly cop, reciting Wade's rights, led his brother over to one of the squad cars. Beside him, Marla began to sob into her hands. Derek was frozen as if made of stone.

"Get me a lawyer!" Wade shouted, and Joel wasn't sure if he was telling him or Marla.

"We're taking him downtown," Halloran said to Marla. "You won't be able to see him tonight. Come down in the morning. In the meantime, your husband gave you some good advice. I'd get an attorney as soon as possible."

10:57 PM

He had asked her name as soon as she had slid into the car.

"Brittany," she said.

"What a beautiful name."

"Thanks."

"Where do you live, Brittany?"

"Munson Street. It's about four blocks—"

"I know where it is."

And when he sailed past Munson Street without even slowing down, he noticed her tense up and shoot him a worried glance. "You just passed it."

He said nothing and kept his eyes on the road.

"Turn around! You passed my street!" She tried the door handle, but it wouldn't budge. It was designed that way. She beat on the glass, but it was shatterproof and her hands bounced off as if they were made of rubber. She had backed up against the door, crying in panic now. "Let me out of here! Let me go!" And with that, she twisted in the seat and kicked him in the side, and his kidney exploded in pain.

They weren't quite at the park yet, but he managed to pull off the road into a secluded drive and throw the car into park. She was still kicking, but he managed to grab her ankles and hold her feet still. He could tell she didn't expect him to be so strong— none of them ever did.

She only screamed once more before he was on top of her, before his fingers wrapped around her throat, cutting off her voice. The gloves were thin, and he could feel her pulse pounding against his fingertips. Pounding and pounding until it began to peter out and she went limp beneath him.

Even through the pain in his side, he managed to drive home and carry her inside with little effort. He stripped her clothes and positioned her inside the freezer like the others, closed the lid and secured the room.

So far he had heard nothing of her disappearance, and he wondered if she had lied about being out past her curfew. Surely by now someone would be missing her. Unless her parents or whoever she lived with was used to her not coming home.

He gazed upon her now in the soft yellow glow of the freezer's light. So beautiful, so perfect. He couldn't imagine anyone not caring about her.

MONDAY, JULY 16

8:45 AM

Joel had been sitting at the table watching Marla on the phone now for thirty minutes. She had been calling and calling, but none of the attorney's offices were open yet. "Just give it up for a few minutes, Marla," he told her. "They'll be in after nine."

Joel had called into work and told Betsy he and Wade had some family issues going on. She had said little, but he could tell she had not been happy. He left her with the promise he would explain everything when he came in later.

In truth, he felt hung over. He had barely slept, and when the room began to lighten around five, he had climbed on out of bed, exhausted but wired. He had allowed himself one cigarette—the first since Friday—but had stubbed it out before he was halfway done with it.

He could not stop thinking about Wade and the visions he had seen. Most of all he could not get the image from his head of Clifton coming at Wade with the bottle. It made him hurt for his brother, knowing what they had both endured over the years, but it also made him angry as hell that he and Wade had never discussed their abuse, had never tried to get past it. But no matter what the two of them had endured, no matter what else Wade had done, he was no murderer. Joel had seen it. Had *felt* it.

Beside him, Derek sat with an untouched glass of orange juice. He had been biting his fingernails again, and Joel noticed with a wince that his thumb was bleeding.

What about Derek? Hadn't he known her as well? Could he have something to do with girl's disappearance? Evidently, the police didn't think so. But sometimes the police could overlook obvious clues. Joel steeled himself for what was to come, then placed a hand on Derek's shoulder.

Instantly he was met with visions and feelings, mostly about girls and cars, and Derek's job at the Dairy Queen, which he evidently hated. He saw Derek talking to the girl at the college, one of many he had also seen Wade rolling around with. But there was nothing else. Derek was innocent as well.

Joel removed his hand and felt the pain between his eyes. Sometimes these episodes left him with migraines, and he was afraid he was getting one now.

Marla slammed the phone down and wiped her eyes on the back of her hand. "Damn lawyers," she muttered. "No one's answering the phone yet."

"Just give them time," Joel said.

She picked up her coffee, then set it back down. "I don't know why I even care." Fresh tears spilled down her face. "I should have left him years ago, while I was still young."

"You don't mean that," Joel said, but after what he had seen in Wade's head yesterday, he knew that she was right.

"He's been out screwing around on me since we got married. I tried to pretend it wasn't happening, that it was just my imagination. And then, when I knew he was really doing it, I told myself it was just temporary. A phase he was going through. I figured he'd settle down after a while, after he got it all out of his system. I should have known." She wiped her face with her sleeve. "And now the dumbass has gone and probably killed somebody. I should be surprised, but I'm not."

Joel rubbed his temples and closed his eyes. Surely his head was going to explode. "He didn't do it, Marla."

"How do you know?" she said, and her voice was sharp.

He opened his eyes and looked at her, meeting her gaze evenly. "I just know," he said.

She took a deep breath. "It doesn't matter. I should just leave his ass in jail. Let him rot in there."

"You can't do that," Joel told her. "He needs you now." He looked at Derek. "He needs all of us."

Marla turned her gaze toward the back door to the outside and took a sip of coffee. "It's just too fucking bad," she said. "When all this is over, I'm gone."

2:17 PM

Wade opened the bottle of water and took a sip. It had been a rough twenty-four hours. Dragged off to jail in front of his family. Suffering a sleepless night in a cell with a passed-out snoring drunk. Having meals with a bunch of punk kids who thought they were hard asses. Meeting with the attorney for the first time—a balding scrap of a boy with a stained shirt and rampant eczema on his elbows—and finding out he had been denied bail. It was almost too much. He was about ready to do anything to get the fuck out of here.

Halloran, the detective across the table from him in the interrogation room, shuffled through his notes. Beside him, the younger detective, Chapman, looked at Wade with cold green eyes, and Wade couldn't help but think his red hair made him look like a big leprechaun. Next to Wade, the fledgling attorney—Wade couldn't even remember his name—scribbled something in a notebook.

"Now," Halloran said, "what's your relationship with Abigail Saunders?"

"I know her," Wade said, "just like I told you yesterday. I met her and her roommate at the Capitol a couple of weeks ago."

"Have the two of you had a sexual relationship?"

"Yes."

"Have you and Miss Mitchell also had a sexual relationship?"

Wade stared at the table, but he had to suppress a slight grin. "Yes."

"Did you ever threaten either of them?"

Wade blew out a breath. "No."

Halloran checked his notes. "Police were called to your house two years ago. Remember that?"

Oh, shit here it comes. "Of course I do." He and Marla had been in one of their many arguments. He had slapped her and she had locked herself in the bedroom and called 911.

"Domestic assault," Halloran said. "Against your wife."

"She dropped the charges."

"But you have a history of violence against women."

"That was a misunderstanding," Wade said. "I never went to jail." He took another sip of water. God, it was hot in this room. "Look me up. I've never been in here or any other jail before."

"We *have* looked you up, Mr. Roberts," the red-haired detective said.

"So you know I'm clean."

Halloran looked at him. "I'm not convinced. I think you killed Abigail Saunders."

Panic struck him. "No!"

The attorney looked up from scribbling. "You have any proof besides the driver's license in his truck?"

Halloran looked at the attorney, but didn't answer him. "It must have really pissed you off to find out you and your son were both interested in the same girl, huh?"

Rage boiled within him. "Leave my son out of this."

"I think you got so pissed that you killed Miss Saunders and dumped her body someplace."

The rage was giving way to exasperation. "I swear to God I had nothing to do with her disappearing. I didn't kill anybody."

"Where is the body, Mr. Roberts? Did you dump it in the river like the others?"

He felt a jolt and looked up at Halloran. "Others? What others?"

The attorney became rigid. "What the hell are you talking about, Lieutenant?"

Halloran looked from the attorney to Wade and back to the attorney. "We recovered Abigail Saunders' driver's license from your truck, but we also found something else. Two hairs. Two blonde hairs."

Wade looked into Halloran's eyes and felt horror washing over him.

"Two blonde hairs that were a match to Sarah Jo McElvoy."

4:29 PM

Marla sat on the porch in the afternoon sun, staring across the road at the field of corn and feeling the glass of Coke and Captain Morgan cold and wet in her hand. She had done it. She had gone and fucking done it. And the asshole had never suspected a thing. He would never have suspected her of all people. No one would have suspected her.

Abby Saunders certainly never suspected anything. Not when she answered her door. Not until Marla asked how long she had been fucking Wade. She had sputtered some excuses then, saying how she didn't know he was married, that he had lied to her. That he had lied to her roommate as well.

And that's when Marla knew the truth. He *had* been fucking both those bitches. The rage had taken over then. Abby ran toward the back of the apartment, but Marla caught her just inside the bedroom door and gave her a punch to the head that sent her sprawling into a bedside table. Abby started pleading with her then. Crying and begging her to stop. But Marla could not control herself. Her anger took over. Beside her was an ironing board. The iron sat atop it. Marla grabbed for it and it went flying, striking Abby in the temple. The girl balled up in pain, then got to her hands and knees to crawl away.

But Marla was too strong for her. Instantly she caught Abby's ankle and shoved her knee into the small of Abby's back, then threw her full weight on it. The girl cried out, but Marla already had the iron's cord wrapped around her throat and was pulling tight. Abby was gasping for breath, and her hands flailed behind her head, clawing frantically at the air. Marla pulled tighter. Sweat was pouring down her face from the effort. She couldn't see Abby's face, but she kept her eyes on one of the girl's ears that stuck out through the mass of curly hair. The car turned bright red, then violet. Gradually, Abby's struggles became weaker and Marla felt her go limp. She continued to pull on the cord long after she thought the girl was dead. She wanted to be sure.

Finally, she fell back off the body and slumped against the bed, exhausted. She wiped the sweat from her face with the tail of her shirt and untangled her legs from Abby's. She watched the girl's back for several minutes before she was convinced she was dead. Then she collapsed on the floor. Her back and shoulders ached, and she rested for a moment to catch her breath and think. And while she lay there, the plan formed in her mind. It was perfect. As long as she didn't get caught.

She pulled the sheet off the unmade bed and clumsily wrapped it around the body. Abby was solid, and the dead weight was nearly impossible to maneuver, especially in the confined area between the dresser and the bed. When the sheet was tucked around the body, Marla looked around the room and spotted Abby's purse on a hook behind the door. She pawed through it until she found a brown leather wallet, and she pulled Abby's license from the holder and stuffed it into her own pocket.

In the darkened living room, she peeked through the curtains to the street below. Night had fallen and the streetlights didn't reach where she had parked the truck at the back of the apartment lot. She watched the street for a moment. No cars passed, and there were no people to be seen. This was her chance.

In the bedroom, she grabbed Abby's body by the ankles and dragged it down the hall toward the door to the apartment. She stuck her head out one more time to make sure the street was clear, then pulled the body out onto the small porch and down the wooden steps. Abby's head knocked against each step on the way down, and for a moment, giddy with nerves, Marla thought she would get the giggles. She took a deep breath and continued down to the gravel lot. At the truck, she lowered the tailgate and hoisted Abby's legs into the bed. Then she grabbed the body under the arms and shoved with all her strength. For a moment she thought her legs would buckle, but she managed to find an extra burst of energy and lift the rest of the body. The sheet had come loose and Abby's hair splayed out across the bed of the truck. Marla climbed up and wrapped the body tighter, then covered it with some of the junk in the pickup's bed. She took a seat on the wheel well and looked at her work. It would be good enough to get out of town, anyway.

She closed the tailgate as quietly as she could, then climbed into the cab. Her hands had begun to shake, but that was from exhaustion. Her mind was calm and clear. She could do this.

She started the truck and backed out of the drive before she turned on the lights, then she headed down the street toward the intersection that would lead her out of the city limits. She watched the body in the rear-view mirror. The junk kept the sheet in place, but she would not breathe easy until she was completely away from the street lights.

At the intersection she had just started to make the turn when the light turned from yellow to red. She almost ran it, but then she caught sight of a police car in the lot of the Hardee's across the street, and she slammed on the brakes. She heard the junk in the bed shift, and her eyes instantly went to the rear-view mirror. With sudden horror, she realized Abby's hair was again visible under the edge of the sheet. She glanced back across the street. The cop car hadn't moved. The driver of the white Grand Am beside her was keeping his eyes on the light. She took a deep breath and gripped the wheel tighter.

The light finally changed, and she made the turn onto the highway toward the darkness at the edge of the city. After a mile or so, the streetlights ended, and she relaxed a little. Ahead was a turnoff onto a dirt lane that wound back into the woods. The road was easy to miss if you weren't looking for it. She slowed and turned off the highway. The thick growth of trees crowded her from both sides and the ruts in the road jarred the truck like an earthquake. She hadn't been back here in years, not since she and Wade came back here to mess around before they were married, but it hadn't changed much.

When she had gone about half a mile, she stopped the truck and climbed out into the heavy night air. The drone of insects blocked all the noise from the highway, and somewhere an owl hooted. It was black as a cave back here, and she stumbled through the tall weeds and undergrowth toward the back of the truck. She opened the tailgate and grabbed the body under the arms. Pulling Abby out was a hell of a lot easier than putting her in, but it was still exhausting.

When the body was on the ground, she rolled it over toward the tree line. Close by were some dead limbs and brush. In the eerie red glow from the taillights, she gathered what loose branches she could and laid them over the crumpled form. When she was satisfied, she shut the tailgate and climbed back into the truck.

At the highway, she turned back toward town. God, she needed a drink, and she wasn't ready to face whatever might be waiting for her at home. On an impulse she wheeled into the lot of O'Connell's Tavern, turned off the engine, and watched the cars in the lot. It was still early, and the rough crowd was at least two hours from showing up.

She grabbed her purse, stepped out of the truck, and entered the bar. Some Trace Adkins song was blaring and everyone seemed preoccupied with conversation. No one looked at her. She headed down a narrow hall to the women's restroom, stepped inside and locked the door.

A stranger stared back at her in the mirror. Her hair was sweaty and tangled and her face was smudged with dirt from the branches in the woods. She quickly washed her face in the sink and patted it dry with some paper towels, then brushed the loose dirt from her shirt; it was dark blue, so it didn't appear too dirty. She ran a brush through her hair and took a deep breath. She at least looked presentable now.

Back at the bar, she ordered a rum and Coke and surveyed the crowd. Good old boys and rough women, all talking loud, laughing, having fun. She took a long sip of her drink and felt the coolness trickle down her throat.

"Don't remember seeing you around here before," a voice drawled next to her.

She turned and was staring into the intense blue eyes of a stubbled masculine face. Short brown hair peeked from beneath his ball cap, and his t-shirt clung so tightly to his frame she could see the outline of his chiseled chest. He was smiling at her. She smiled back. "I don't come here much," she said, and took another sip of her rum and Coke.

"Yeah, I think I'd remember you," he said.

She realized he was flirting with her, and she felt a surge of adrenaline, like lightning through her body. She could have him, she thought. She could take him outside to the truck right now and climb on top of him in the seat and go at it. And maybe when she was done with him, she'd come back inside and grab another guy. And then she would go home and tell Wade all about it. Wouldn't that just be fitting?

Instead, she drained her glass, paid for her drink and left without another word. Right now she just wanted to get home and stand in a hot shower.

She drove back the way she had come, past the hidden dirt lane, and turned up the road to home. She saw that Derek was already home, and she was surprised when she looked at the clock on the dash. She had been gone almost six hours.

She stepped out of the truck, suddenly wobbly from exhaustion and the rum, and was just about to head into the house when she remembered Abby's license in her pocket. She pulled it out, rubbed both sides of it with her shirt and flicked it into the darkness under the seat. Let the bastard explain that one.

And now she stretched in the sun, feeling the

warmth deep in her muscles, and closed her eyes. Tonight she just might head back to O'Connell's. She
might find the guy in the ball cap. And this time she
wouldn't run away.

4:45 PM

Joel had just pulled up to the stoplight when his cell-
phone rang. He looked at the screen and felt a rush
when he saw Dana's name. "Hey, girl."

"How's it going?"

"Oh, you know. Okay, I guess."

"What's new with Wade?"

He filled her in with what he knew regarding Wade
being denied bail. "I think something else is going on,
though," he said. "I don't believe Marla's told me everything."

"Why would she keep anything from you?"

"I don't know." Truth was, he wondered if Marla
was involved somehow with the girl's disappearance.
He had seen how Wade treated her, and if she had the
chance to even the score, he thought she might take it.
"I'm on my way home right now. I'm going to stop by
there and see if she heard anything else from the attorney today. I know this has all got to be a big
misunderstanding."

"Why don't you let me fix dinner for you tonight?"

He smiled. The traffic light turned green, and he
pulled on through the intersection. "That's awfully
sweet of you," he said. "What time do you want me?"

"Why don't I come over to your place?" she said.

"I'll bring all the stuff and fix it there."

"Sounds good."

"You like spaghetti?"

"This is sounding better all the time," he said.

"I'll try to be there about six-thirty."

"I'll be waiting."

He hung up the phone stared at the road ahead. He could feel the silly grin that was plastered to his face. He imagined what he looked like to other drivers and that made him laugh. Tonight would be just what he needed to get his mind off everything else.

5:03 PM

Halloran leaned back in his chair, blew out a breath and closed his eyes. Tomorrow they would formally charge Wade Roberts in connection with Abigail Saunders' disappearance and the murder of Sarah Jo McElvoy. Even though most of their evidence was circumstantial, Halloran was sure they could get a conviction. They had not even told Roberts yet; the plan was to meet with him and his attorney, then hold a press conference and make the announcement.

It had been a godawful couple of weeks. No one in the department had slept much since Sarah Jo's body had been discovered, and now that they were all seeing some light at the end of the tunnel, a sense of relief had swept through the office. People seemed a little happier, a little friendlier. It was almost like Christmas.

"Taking a nap?"

Halloran opened his eyes. Chapman stood in the

doorway with a smirk on his freckled face. "I could sleep for two weeks," Halloran said.

"I know what you mean," Chapman told him.

Halloran rubbed his eyes. "I really hope this is the end of it. The only thing that would make this any sweeter would be a full confession."

"Don't think that's gonna happen," Chapman said.

"You're probably right."

"Hey, how about you come over to our house for dinner tonight?"

"I couldn't do that."

"Why not?" Chapman said. "I'll call Sheri and tell her you're coming over. I'm sure she won't mind."

Honestly, all Halloran really wanted to do was go home, strip down to his boxers, and relax in front of the television with his cat and a cold Bud Light. But he hated to turn down any invitation for a free home-cooked meal. "Okay, you twisted my arm."

Chapman gave him a wide grin. "Great. You head on over there, and I'll call Sheri and tell her to meet you at the front door with a monster margarita."

Halloran laughed. "Just a beer will do."

5:10 PM

Joel pulled the cable truck into Wade's driveway and immediately knew something was different. Marla was sprawled in a lawn chair on the porch, and you didn't have to be psychic to know she had been drinking. Her eyes were glassy and unfocussed, and her face was colored with a flush Joel knew wasn't sunburn. "What's up?" he said, sliding out of the truck.

"Not a goddamned thing," Marla said, and Joel winced at her slurred speech. "How's my favorite brother-in-law?"

"Any more news from Wade?" Joel asked. "You talk to the attorney again today?"

"No." She turned up her glass and Joel caught the strong whiff of alcohol. Marla had evidently been at this for a long while.

"Did you try to call him?"

"What for? I'm sure he'll call if he knows anything."

Joel shrugged. "Okay, whatever." He turned to go. "Well, let me know if you hear anything else."

"Hey, Joel," Marla said, "when all this is over, we should go on a trip. You and me and Derek. All three of us."

"Sure."

"We should go to Disney World. I always wanted to take Derek to Disney World."

"Whatever you want."

"We'd have a real good time," she said. She reached over and grabbed his arm.

And suddenly he saw it all. He saw the struggle with Abby, Marla strangling her with the iron cord, then dumping her on a secluded road. He saw the years of beatings and verbal lashings from Wade, the brutality and cruelty, and he knew his fear was real. She had set Wade up. Had wanted to see him punished. And she had done it the only way that would keep him from retaliating against her. And she was proud of it. She had used Wade's own indiscretions against him.

He backed off from her, staring at her. He was sure his face gave away what he knew, but Marla was too drunk to notice. "I've got to go," he managed to sputter. He whirled around and headed to the truck.

Inside the cab, he pulled Halloran's card from his wallet and dialed the police station with shaking fingers. But the call was answered by Chapman, and Joel remembered he was the younger detective he had seen yesterday. "Is the lieutenant in?" Joel asked.

"Already gone for the day," Chapman said. "Anything I can do for you?"

"This is Joel Roberts. I've got some. . . information about my brother's case. It's urgent. I need to talk to him."

"Tell you what," Chapman said, "I'm getting ready to leave here myself. How about I just swing by your place on my way home and talk to you there?"

"Sure," Joel said. Talking to Chapman surely would be just as good as talking to Halloran.

5:37 PM

Halloran pulled into the drive at Chapman's modest brick house. Even though the grass needed to be mowed and a couple of toys littered the lawn, the place looked comfortable and homey. He thought of his tiny apartment across town, with no one waiting there for him but Mel, and he suddenly felt old and worn-out. He knew he was just tired. After tomorrow he would finally be able to get some rest.

Sheri met him at the door before he could even ring the bell. "Come on in," she said, and stepped back to let him enter. She was blond and petite and moved with the grace of a pixie.

Halloran sniffed the air. "Something smells good."

"Enchiladas," she said.

He looked about for Chapman's daughter. "Where's Isabel?"

"Taking a nap," Sheri said. "She'll probably wake up just in time to be cranky for dinner."

Halloran followed her into the kitchen. "Hope you don't mind me coming over like this."

"Not a problem," Sheri said. She stirred the rice on the stove. "I'm used to John bringing home strays." They laughed, and then she whirled around. "Oh, I forgot. He just called and said he's going to be a little while. Said he would tell you about it when he got here." She opened the fridge. "You want a beer? You can relax for a while in the den until dinner's ready."

"Sounds great, thanks." He smiled. Sheri certainly knew how to take care of a man.

5:57 PM

Joel opened the door just as the detective stepped up onto the porch. "Saw your car pull in," he said. "Thanks for coming out here."

"My pleasure," Chapman said. He stepped into the kitchen and looked around.

Joel had been tidying up since he got home, preparing for Dana, so at least the place didn't look too bad.

He motioned toward the table. "Have a seat."

"Thanks." Chapman slid into a chair and pulled out a small memo pad.

"Would you like something to drink?" Joel asked. "Coke or water or anything?"

Chapman licked his lips. "I'd love some water if it's not too much trouble."

Joel pulled two bottles from the fridge and offered one to Chapman. "I never drink the tap water," he said. "When I was growing up we had well water, and it was good and sweet. Then when the county came along and put in lines, the water always had a funny taste after that."

Chapman unscrewed the cap and drank thirstily. "Oh, that's great," he said. "Been dry all day." He set the bottle down and pulled a pen from his jacket pocket. "So what did you need to talk with us about?"

Joel hesitated. He wasn't quite sure how to go about this without sounding crazy. "It's my sister-in-law," he said. "I think she had something to do with that Saunders girl's disappearance."

Chapman's expression became puzzled. "What makes you think that?"

This was where Joel had no idea what to say. He could tell the truth and risk being thought of as a nut, a hindrance to law enforcement. Or he could lie. And even if he lied, he would still be doing the right thing in the end. Right? He looked at Chapman. "She told me," he said.

Chapman stared at him for a moment. "She *told* you? What did she say?"

Joel looked at the table. "She said she did it. She killed her."

For a second, Chapman didn't move. He sat with his mouth open, pinching his bottom lip. He shook his head and reached for his water. Instead of grabbing it, he grazed it with his knuckles, and the bottle tipped over. Water flowed over the table. "Oh, I'm so sorry," Chapman said, rising from his seat.

"I got it," Joel said. He grabbed some paper towels and began to blot the puddle.

"Here, I'll help," Chapman said. He reached for the paper towels and brushed his hand against Joel's arm.

6:10 PM

Halloran sat in Chapman's den, sipping his beer and flipping through the television stations. God, he hated TV. He stopped on the news—the channel out of Springfield. They'd have a big top story tomorrow. He looked at the anchor, Randy Webber, with his blow-dried hair and shit-eating smile and felt sickened at the thought of him delivering that news with unseemly excitement.

He stood and wandered over to the shelves on the back wall. The bottom was full of board books for Isabel, and he laughed as he saw a couple of Cheerios wedged between the covers. There was a set of encyclopedias—no doubt John's or Sheri's from high school. And someone really liked Stephen King. Hardbacks. They were book club editions, but hardbacks just the same.

He had just taken another sip of beer and turned back toward the television when something in the corner between the bookshelf and the paneled wall caught his eye. A black case with a silver latch. He pulled it out and opened it and suddenly the beer was like acid in his stomach. He was staring at a clarinet. And even before he looked at the nametag, he knew what he would see.

Sarah Jo McElvoy.

He pulled his phone from his pocket to call the station. He had to know where Chapman had gone.

6:17 PM

Joel pulled his hand back.

It was as if he had plunged his arm into a mass of writhing, slimy worms. And worse was what he had seen. The girls—Sarah Jo McElvoy. Carmelita Santos. Another named Brittany. He backed away from the table, not wanting to meet Chapman's eyes.

"Mr. Roberts?" Chapman said, and his voice seemed far away. "What's wrong?"

Joel looked at him then. His eyes were so green. So innocent. Surely he was wrong. This had to be a mistake. Maybe it was leftover from where Chapman had touched someone else. But deep down he knew. It was the truth. He continued to back away. And before he could stop himself, before the reasoning part of his brain could take over, he blurted out, "You killed them."

Chapman froze. "What did you say?"

Joel didn't move. He continued to stare at Chapman. He realized Chapman's eyes didn't look innocent at all. They had suddenly become cold and dark. Joel took another step back and felt the counter against the small of his back. He was cornered.

Chapman kept his gaze steady as he reached inside his suit jacket and brought out his gun. He pointed it at Joel. "Tell me again what you said."

Joel's mouth was dry as sand. "I said. . . you killed them."

Chapman moved around the table and took a step toward Joel. "Killed who?"

"Those girls. You did, didn't you? You murdered them."

Chapman shook his head. "What are you talking about?"

"You killed them. You strangled them. Then you froze them. Then you dumped them in the river."

Chapman was closer now. He leveled his gun at Joel's chest. His voice was a whisper. "How do you know that? Who have you been talking to?"

The back door swung open and Dana called out, "Joel?"

Chapman turned toward the sound.

Joel flew at him, grabbing for him, but Chapman was too quick. He sidestepped out of the way, and Joel crashed to the floor. And before Joel could utter a sound, Chapman had Dana's arm and the gun pointed at her. She screamed, dropping her bags and scattering tomatoes and cans across the floor.

She looked at Joel, her eyes round and scared.

"What's going on?"

Joel shook his head. "I'm sorry, Dana."

"Your boyfriend knows a lot," Chapman said. "I don't know how, but he knows too much for his own good." He pulled Dana toward the door. "We're going for a little ride."

Dana grabbed for the door frame as Joel struggled to his feet. "Joel!"

Chapman turned and fired, shattering the window over the sink, and Joel ducked back to the floor.

"Joel!" Dana screamed again, but Chapman had already dragged her out to the back porch.

Joel grabbed a chair to pull himself up with, and that was when he saw the blood on his shoulder. Suddenly numb with fear, he touched the torn red-soaked sleeve and felt the raw flesh where Chapman's bullet had grazed him. It was the jolt he needed to get to his feet and lunge for the door.

Just as he crossed the kitchen, a dark sedan and two patrol cars wheeled into the drive. Chapman and Dana stood with their backs to him on the steps, facing Halloran and the other cops as they emerged.

Halloran raised his hands. "John! I found Sarah Jo's clarinet. What the fuck? What the *fuck!*"

The other officers had taken positions behind their open doors. All of them had their weapons pointed at Chapman and Dana.

Halloran continued to move toward the house. "Why? I don't understand. How could you do it? How could you kill them?"

Chapman shook his head. "Why does anyone do

anything?"

"I trusted you," Halloran said. "You lied to me. You planted evidence. You tried to frame innocent people."

"It was all so easy to do. No one stopped me. No one asked any questions. Not even you. Not even Sheri. She never once wanted to know what I was doing out in the shed behind the house. Never."

Halloran took another step closer and Chapman shoved the gun to Dana's head. Dana was whimpering, and the fact that Joel couldn't see her face made it worse. "Don't come any closer," Chapman said. "I'll kill her."

Halloran blew out a breath. "How do you think this is going to end, John? It's over. Give it up."

Just at that moment, Joel locked glances with Halloran, and Halloran looked away. Had Chapman noticed? If so, he gave no indication.

Barry's words echoed through Joel's head: *Tackle him.*

But Chapman held a tight grip around Dana's neck. Surely if Joel grabbed him now the three of them would plunge off the porch and break Dana's neck. Or Chapman's gun would go off.

Even if you think it's too dangerous. Do it anyway.

Joel slipped through the door, keeping his eyes on the back of Chapman's head.

Halloran raised his hands again. "Let her go, John."

"Back off, Mike," Chapman said.

"Let her go and I'll do everything I can to keep you out of the electric chair. I'll testify you were sick. You didn't know what you were doing."

"I knew what I was doing," Chapman said. "Every time."

Chapman had moved slightly away from Dana and Joel saw his grip loosen.

You'll know when.

Before he could talk himself out of it, Joel launched himself at Chapman and Dana. He grabbed the smaller man around the waist and the three of them plummeted off the steps to the ground below. Joel felt something pop in his shoulder as they hit.

The cops were on them at once. Chapman was gasping; the landing had knocked the wind out of him. Two officers had him cuffed in seconds and were leading him back to one of the patrol cars.

Instantly, Dana was beside him. "Joel! Oh, my god, are you all right?"

He realized she was touching him and he saw that everything else within her was silenced by her concern for him. He managed a smile. "I'll be okay."

Halloran squatted in front of them. "Mr. Roberts, that was either very stupid or very brave, I'm not sure which."

Joel laughed. "A little of both, I think."

Halloran gave him an approving nod. "In any event, thank you." He stood and glanced over his shoulder at the activity behind him. "You two sit tight. We'll have an ambulance here shortly." He headed back toward the patrol car where Chapman sat in the back seat like a statue.

"My God, Joel," Dana said, looking at him. "You're

bleeding!"

"I think I got shot when he was taking you out," he said. The swirling lights on the police cars were starting to nauseate him. He rested his forehead against his knee. Everything was starting to spin.

She touched his shoulder gently, and her eyes were soft and round with worry. "Oh, my God, Joel," she said again, whispering this time.

"You're gorgeous," he told her. And everything went black.

SATURDAY, AUGUST 4

12:38 PM

Halloran put the last of his bags in the back of the Trailblazer and shut the hatch. It was beautiful out. The velvet breeze stirred the summer air and brought the sounds of lawnmowers and kids playing at the park. It would be a fine day to drive. He hadn't driven his own vehicle in a while, and he was looking forward to getting behind the wheel and letting the Chevrolet stretch its legs on the interstate. He hoped to make the outskirts of Kansas City before stopping for the night.

Since Chapman's arrest and confession, Halloran had been buried in paperwork and red tape. He had been questioned extensively, as had Chief Pettus and every other officer that had worked with Chapman. No one had seen it coming. The idea that one of their own had committed those atrocious acts was horrifying.

No one, however, had been more devastated than

Sheri Chapman. The realization of what had been going on in the shed behind their house, what was stored
in the old second-hand freezer, was more than she could
take. She and Isabel had left the house and were now
living with Sheri's parents in Springfield.

Halloran understood the need to get away. When the
investigation wrapped up, the first thing he did was call
Mark Miller in Wyoming. Yes, the invitation to visit
was still open. Yes, the fishing was good. And yes,
there was a spare bed Halloran could have for a few
weeks. Miller hadn't asked any questions and Halloran
hadn't offered any reasons. There would be plenty of
time to fill him in later.

Brooks pulled up and parked his Impala behind the
SUV. He stepped out, straightening his ball cap. He
was wearing jeans and a Jason Aldean t-shirt. It was
the first time Halloran had ever seen him out of uniform. "Thought you forgot," Halloran told him.

"You know my daughter wouldn't let me forget anything this important," Brooks said.

Halloran picked up the pet carrier and Mel meowed
at him through the wire door. "Just for a little while,"
Halloran said. "You'll get to play with another cat for
six whole weeks." He handed the carrier to Brooks.
"Tell your daughter to take good care of him."

Brooks took the handle. "You sure I can't talk you
out of this crazy thing?"

Halloran chuckled. "Positive." He leaned back
against the Trailblazer. "I need this. I need to clear my
head. When I come back to work I want a clean start."
He looked at Brooks. "With my new partner."

Brooks gave him a glance, then looked away with a shy grin. "Pettus hasn't made the decision yet."

"He will," Halloran said. "You're a good cop, Greg. And you'll make a damn fine detective. Pettus knows that, too."

"Thanks," said Brooks. "I appreciate that." He stuck out his hand and Halloran shook it. "Take care."

Halloran nodded. "I'll see you." He bent down and peered into Mel's face in the carrier. "See you in six weeks, you stupid cat."

He climbed into the Trailblazer, started it, and pulled out, heading toward the interstate. He had an eight-hour drive ahead of him, a full tank of gas, and some good eighties rock on the satellite radio.

He was already feeling better.

3:45 PM

After a light lunch and an early matinee, Dana had wanted to go out to the park and enjoy the outdoors. After being cooped up in the house for two weeks, Joel was more than happy to go along. His arm was still in a sling, more for the break he sustained when he tackled Chapman than the gunshot, and though everything appeared to be healing nicely, he had been told to expect some type of surgery in his future. Monday he planned on returning to work, and Betsy had already assured him he could have some light duty desk work for a while. There would be no climbing cable towers for several weeks.

Marla had crumpled fairly quickly when faced with

the evidence in Abby Saunders' murder, and now she sat in the county jail awaiting her sentence—the same jail she had tried to send Wade to. Although he understood her motives, twisted as they were, Joel was hard pressed to feel any sympathy for her. He knew that her attorney would play up the abused spouse angle, even though Wade was not the direct target of her actions.

For his part, Wade had stayed closer to home the past couple of weeks, although Joel wondered how long that would last. He and Derek were spending a lot of time together, and that had to be good for both of them. He knew Derek faced a hard road ahead, and having Wade around, even if he hadn't been much of a father, was better than the alternative.

Beside him, Dana took his hand. He was becoming used to it now, this touching. He was able to control the feelings, to minimize the barrage of sensations that until now had always overwhelmed him. He supposed it had been a matter of desensitizing himself, something he had never had the opportunity to work on until he met Dana. But being with her day after day, touching her—tentatively at first—had given him the courage to explore those feelings without fear.

"What'cha thinking about?" she asked.

He shrugged. "Just everything."

"That's a lot to think about."

They reached one of the big oaks and stretched out in its shade. Joel leaned back against the trunk, and Dana cuddled against him, her head resting on his chest. Across the grassy knoll, two little girls played on the swings, giggling and squealing as they rose higher.

Suddenly he understood how they felt—light and free and happy with no worry and only the *now* to contemplate. He wanted this moment to last forever.

He looked down at Dana and her eyes met his. And then he was kissing her, tasting her. And he could see everything—her hopes, her dreams, her fears. Her deepest secrets and private thoughts. He could see into her soul. And he knew this was where he wanted to spend the rest of his life.

ABOUT THE AUTHOR

Award-winning author and sometime banker Will Overby has spent over thirty years in the boardrooms and glass offices of retail banking. Between dodging mergers and drafting policies he publishes novels.

He lives along the Ohio River in western Kentucky where mysteries still abound and the tradition of story-telling is as strong as ever.

A graduate of Indiana University, Will is an avid Hoosiers football fan.

Connect with him on his website, *willoverby.com*, on Facebook, or follow him on Twitter (@Will_Overby).

www.ingramcontent.com/pod-product-compliance
Lightning Source LLC
Chambersburg PA
CBHW021645260626
47154CB00017BA/2487